Murder of
the Maestro

Georgie Shaw Cozy Mystery #6

Anna Celeste Burke

MURDER OF THE MAESTRO

Copyright © 2018 Anna Celeste Burke

http://desertcitiesmystery.com

Cover Design by Anna Celeste Burke
Photo © © Sagasan | Dreamstime.com

ISBN-13: **978-1979139687**
ISBN-10: **1979139687**

Books by USA Today Bestselling Author, Anna Celeste Burke

A Dead Husband Jessica Huntington Desert Cities Mystery #1

A Dead Sister Jessica Huntington Desert Cities Mystery #2

A Dead Daughter Jessica Huntington Desert Cities Mystery # 3

A Dead Mother Jessica Huntington Desert Cities Mystery #4

A Dead Cousin Jessica Huntington Desert Cities Mystery #5 [2018]

Love A Foot Above the Ground Prequel to the Jessica Huntington Desert Cities Mystery Series

~~~~~

Cowabunga Christmas! Corsario Cove Cozy Mystery #1

Gnarly New Year Corsario Cove Cozy Mystery #2

Heinous Habits, Corsario Cove Cozy Mystery #3

Radical Regatta, Corsario Cove Cozy Mystery #4 [2018]

~~~~~

Murder at Catmmando Mountain Georgie Shaw Cozy Mystery #1

Love Notes in the Key of Sea Georgie Shaw Cozy Mystery #2

All Hallows' Eve Heist Georgie Shaw Cozy Mystery #3

A Merry Christmas Wedding Mystery Georgie Shaw Cozy Mystery #4

Murder at Sea of Passenger X Georgie Shaw Cozy Mystery #5

Murder of the Maestro Georgie Shaw Cozy Mystery #6

A Tango Before Dying Georgie Shaw Cozy Mystery #7 [2018]

~~~~~

DEDICATION

To the man who makes the music in my life!

CONTENTS

ACKNOWLEDGMENTS

Thanks to my husband who supported my efforts to get this book written and produced even while fighting a prolonged illness. He's my inspiration for Detective Jack Wheeler as well as the other strong, determined decent and loving men who appear in the books I write. I'm blessed to have him in my life.

Thanks, as well, to Ying Cooper for tackling another proofreading job with a deadline looming. Her skill as an editor, confidence, and grace under fire are attributes that I greatly appreciate.

Gratitude to Andra Weis for taking on the task of reading *Murder of the Maestro* before it had been edited. I'm grateful for her willingness to take this task on at the last minute and for her invaluable feedback. And, to Peggy Hyndman for her keen eye and quick read that spotted a couple of snafus, too!

I'm a fortunate author to have this kind of support and don't take it for granted for even a minute! That goes for all the readers who read and review this book and the others I write. THANK YOU!!

1 ON THE ROCKS

My heart raced when my cell phone belted out the Marvelous Marley World ringtone before dawn. Like a cult member, my brain involuntarily chanted along with the familiar tune: *"It's a marvelous world, a Marvelous Marley World."* Not one word of that could be true. A phone call at the crack of dawn is never marvelous, is it?

I can't entirely blame that ringtone for my racing heart. Seconds before my phone blared, Miles bellowed. I don't know how he does it, but my Siamese cat anticipates lots of the action that goes on around here. That's especially true about doorbells, alarms, or phones about to ring. Is it an acute sense of hearing he possesses that picks up tiny sounds humans can't detect, or does he have an uncanny ability to anticipate trouble?

Not just one, but two Siamese cats stared at me now. Their blue eyes shimmered in the shadowy light cast by the creeping dawn as I typed in my passcode. Not fast enough since that theme song played again.

1

Mighty-mouth, who regularly demonstrates that naming him after the jazz trumpet player, Miles Davis, was a good choice, sat Sphinxlike. The lovely Ella posed next to him. My cats who love routine almost as much as their creature comforts, were not happy with the disruption—as if I were the one who'd raised the alarm!

"Don't blame me," I said, answering the call before I had to listen to the ringtone a third time.

"Why would I do that?" my sleepy husband asked. "Carol did it, didn't she?" My clever, technologically savvy Executive Assistant takes great delight in playing pranks on me, like changing the ringtone on my phone. I'm a diehard fan of all the marvels at Marvelous Marley World, but even I have my limits. That ringtone had to go.

"Yes, sweetheart, but I wasn't talking to you." I gave Jack a reassuring pat. "I'm trying to get the cats to stop eyeing me like I'm up to no good." That I was chatting with my cats didn't strike my new husband as odd at all. I catch him talking to them too, even though he's only been "owned by cats" for a year. I preferred the conversation I was having with them to the one that began the moment my caller had me on the line.

"Slow down, Max, please!" I implored my frantic boss moments later. He was beside himself with news that his "old friend," Dave Rollins, was missing. I could understand his concern since Max's old friend is well into his seventies. Maximillian Marley, the founder of Marvelous Marley World is no spring chicken either. He needed to calm down, not that I could make that happen.

Max has had decades of practice running around with his hair on fire when he's worried or upset. You never could tell how seriously to take his fretfulness. His tantrums are legendary, too. I could barely handle the panicky episodes and tantrum-throwing when fully awake. I wasn't sure what I might do if he went into Rumpelstiltskin mode before six a.m. and without my usual fortification with strong coffee.

When Jack heard me utter Max's name, he covered his head with a pillow and turned over with his back to me. Both cats swung their heads in Jack's direction, their eyes boring into his back freeing me for a moment from their steely-blue gazes. I peeked out through the large bedroom windows and scanned the horizon where the Pacific Ocean meets the sky. The glow of the morning sun had just begun to cast its light on the placid sea. A measure of calm returned as I took a deep breath.

"Start over, please, and tell me everything that's happened."

According to my distraught boss, someone had called the police sending them to Dave Rollins' home several hours ago. Music was blaring from open windows in the middle of the night. Every light in the house was on, as if he was having a party.

There wasn't a party. In fact, no one was home. Not even Dave Rollins, master musician, composer, and, until recently, Chief Creative Officer for the Marvelous Marley World Music Group. When the well-known local celebrity didn't answer the door, the police pounded on the door loudly, announced themselves, and then went inside. The door was already unlocked, and not even completely latched, so they had no trouble getting in once that's what they'd decided to do.

"It sounds horrible. Just horrible what someone did to his place!" Max cried and then rambled on about what he meant by that. "His magnificent home is in disarray as if it's been searched. Vandalized, too. The police are searching for the intruder, but what good will that do? They should be looking for Dave."

"Let's hope the maestro has gone off somewhere, even if it's just for the weekend. That would explain why someone broke into his home without Dave calling the police himself."

"You know Dave, he'd never just take off. Even if he did, why wouldn't he answer his cell phone when I called?"

I didn't take the bait by responding to that question. A dozen reasons sprang to mind for not taking a call from "Mad" Max Marley; the early hour only one of them. Max didn't give me time to say anything anyway.

"I couldn't believe it when the Lost Hills police officer had the gall to suggest Dave had simply gone off on a jaunt. Lost Hills is the right place for that officer, alright, since he's the one who's lost! To treat Dave's sudden disappearance as if he were an errant teenager staying out past curfew or a college kid off on a backpacking trip is reprehensible! With his house in the state they found it, how could anyone say a thing like that?"

"I understand you're upset. I'm sure the Lost Hills police officer was trying to reassure you since they couldn't possibly have enough information to even guess at what went on there. A burglary must be high on their list. If Dave had been home at the time of the incident, he would have locked himself in his panic room, and called the police, don't you think?"

I tried to sound calm and confident as I asked Max that question. I skimmed over the fact that before I asked Max to start over he'd mentioned that the police suggested a struggle might have contributed to the wreckage found at Dave Rollins' home. That raised the specter of a home invasion, kidnapping, or worse. Apparently, Max was having a conversation with himself since the next words out of his mouth had nothing to do with my question about Dave Rollins using his panic room.

"No blood, no body, indeed! That still doesn't mean no foul play!"

"What do you mean no blood, no body?" Jack, who had already taken the pillow off his head and rolled back over to face me, made eye contact when he heard that question. I gave him a little shrug in return.

That was it. Detective Jack Wheeler tossed his pillow to the foot of the bed. The cats bolted as Jack sprang to his feet, grabbed his phone, and placed a call. I heard him asking for someone with the Los Angeles County Sheriff's Department at the Lost Hills/Malibu station.

"That's what the young fool from Lost Hills told me. I demanded they organize a search for Dave Rollins immediately. Since there was no blood and no body at the location, they had no reason to put out an APB, or whatever they call it, for Dave Rollins or anyone else. He actually told me to cool it!"

Uh-oh, I thought. *That sounded like an order. Max*

loves to give orders, but no one tells him what to do. An inspired dreamer who'd invented a private world with an odd assortment of fantastical creatures that inhabited cartoons, movies, theme parks, and resorts, Max often behaved as though he ruled the real world too.

"Hang on a second while I tell Jack what no blood, no body means." I relayed the information quickly just as our morning alarm went off. I shut it off, rolled out of bed, and slipped on my robe while continuing my conversation with Max.

"Dave didn't say a word to Jack or me about planning to go anywhere. I take it he didn't tell you he had travel plans, either, and there's no way the mess at his house could be from packing in a hurry."

"No, he did not! In fact, he told me all he wanted to do for the foreseeable future was sit and ponder the music of the waves or some nonsense like that. I tried to get him to commit to creating a special composition for our Catmmando Tom Jubilee Commemoration in two years and he turned me down!"

Imagine that, I thought, keeping my sarcasm to myself. "Well, it wouldn't be much of a retirement if he started on a new project right away. That sounds like an ambitious one, too," I said, walking down the hall to the kitchen. I was desperate to make a pot of coffee. I'm pretty sure what I heard in response to my statement was a harrumph from Max.

By the time I reached the kitchen, Miles and Ella were already seated on barstools at the large granite kitchen island, ready to assume their supervisory roles. For the moment, they patiently waited for service—morning treats of gourmet canned food, tuna, or turkey.

"Dave has never been one to shun ambition," Max sputtered.

"Uh huh," I murmured to Max as I multi-tasked in my quasi-conscious state. I pulled items from the cupboards and began my morning rituals with my mind still operating in low gear.

I went over my most recent encounter with Dave. Jack and I had just seen him the night before at an elaborate gala held in his honor to celebrate his retirement. He'd been the consummate showman, as always. With his mass of white hair, longer and even more unruly than Max's, he was the quintessential orchestra director decked out in a traditional tuxedo with the long tails.

He'd been presented with a lovely gold conductor's baton and had wielded it with apparent delight as he posed for pictures with Marvelous Marley World colleagues. There was no hint that anything was wrong as he clowned around with some of our associates dressed as beloved Marvelous Marley World characters. A well-known ladies' man, he'd also flirted his way through a gaggle of adoring women—young and old alike.

Over the years, the maestro had composed dozens of songs, many of which had become identified with the iconic characters for whom they'd been written. He'd also created lovely arrangements of his work and the work of others, scored live-action feature films, full-length animated films as well as cartoons and film shorts. Those efforts had earned him Oscars, Grammys, and Emmys along with other honors and awards. Many of his tunes were as catchy as the Marvelous Marley World theme song he'd penned early in his career when only a handful of people worked in what eventually became the Marvelous Marley World Music Group.

When the aroma of fresh-ground coffee hit me, I realized that Max had been speaking. There had been more after my "uh huh," and I'd missed it. The last few words that made their way into my brain had something to do with "a jubilee like no other." If I had to guess, I'd say that Max had just delivered a long soliloquy about the project he envisioned to commemorate Catmmando Tom's debut decades ago. That must have included a reference to the great honor it would have been for Dave Rollins to participate. Maybe the maestro made a hasty departure for parts unknown, trying to outrun Max's inability to take no for an answer.

"I hear you," I muttered, sort of lying. "I'm sure he understood the opportunity you were offering him. Dave told us last night how much he was looking forward to doing nothing for a while." Before he could respond, I changed the subject. "How did you find out that Dave was missing? Did the police call you?"

"Pat contacted me. One of Dave's neighbors knows she's been his Personal Assistant for years and called her to complain about the loud music rather than filing a complaint with the police. When she couldn't get Dave to answer his phone, she drove to Malibu and found the police already in Dave's house after other neighbors had complained. She called me hoping Dave had changed his mind and decided to spend the weekend here at my house to discuss the jubilee project. When I got off the phone with Pat, I went right to the source, and called the officer on the scene rather than rely solely upon her version of events. That's what I want you and Jack to do."

"Sure, I'll give Pat a call."

"Yes, yes, of course. You should do that right away. I've told Pat that she is not to leave Dave's house under any circumstance. What's more important is that you two go to Malibu while Pat and the police are still there. That's the only way to get to the bottom of this impossible situation right away. Don't let them give you the run around either. I want answers!"

Let the eye-rolling begin, I thought, glad that Max couldn't see my reaction.

"We can't just barge in there. Jack's trying to reach someone with the County Sheriff's Department, but Malibu's outside his jurisdiction."

"I don't care about jurisdictions. You two need to get over there now!" That order had been delivered loud enough to rattle my nerves.

Here comes Rumpelstiltskin, I thought as I held the phone away from my ear. I could picture Max jumping up and down like that angry little fairytale troll.

Tempted to lay my phone down on the counter, I struggled to pop the top on a can of cat food with one hand. Miles bellowed, either in response to the commotion on the other end of my phone, or in irritation at my lack of agility while doing something as simple as opening a can of cat food. He does not appreciate slow or sloppy service. Just then, Jack stepped up behind me and wrapped his arms around me.

"Tell Max we'll get there as soon as we can." My mouth fell open when Jack said that. I turned to face my husband who awed me, once again, with his ability to cope with mornings and unwelcome surprises. Clean-shaven and fully-dressed, he was ready to roll.

"Tell Jack I said thanks," Max demanded in a calmer tone.

"You heard that?" I asked Max.

"Sure, I did. I'm old but there's nothing wrong with my hearing," he sniffed indignantly.

"He heard that," I told Jack. *There's no way out now*, I mused silently.

"I've got this. Go get dressed. Treats!" He yelled to the delight of both cats. Then he took the can of cat food from me, leaned in and whispered. "They found a body. Not in the house, but on the rocks below. Let's find out more before you break the news to Max," he whispered. "My contact from the Lost Hills station tells me Pat Dolan could benefit from the support of a friend."

"Bye, Max! Talk to you later," Jack hollered as he ended the phone call.

I dashed down the hall to dress, still woefully caffeine deprived. My head was spinning. Why not? Events around me were moving way too fast. A pit formed in my stomach as Jack's words sank in. A body on the rocks below the maestro's magnificent Malibu Cliffs estate could only mean one thing. Dave Rollins was dead.

2 PRELUDE TO ROMANCE

Sunlight sparkled on the water below the cliffs as Jack and I stood overlooking the beach near Dave Rollins' Malibu estate. The view was usually quite lovely. This morning, the area off to the left at the foot of the cliffs had been cordoned off by the police as the coroner and crime scene investigators—CSIs—clambered over the rocks at awkward angles. Their movements were disturbingly crablike.

Light cast by the full moon the night before must not have been enough for anyone to see the body on the rocks below if someone had been around to see it. That explained why no one had found the maestro when Max spoke to the police demanding information about the whereabouts of his longtime friend. Despite how disgruntled Max was when he called me, it was fortunate the police investigation got underway as early as it did. That was the best I could do to find a silver lining in this dark cloud.

"I guess it's a good thing Dave's neighbors complained, isn't it?"

"Yes. Those calls put Dave Rollins' disappearance on the record sooner than it would have been otherwise. It got Pat over here quick, too. If she hadn't insisted the police search for him on the beach, it's possible the tide would have carried his body out to sea. Without a body, the maestro's disappearance could have remained a missing persons case rather than becoming a homicide investigation. A sad story either way, as you know all too well, my love."

Jack was right. There was a hint of déjà vu in all of this, accentuated by a chilling ocean breeze that swirled around us. I'd lived through something similar in my youth. An attack on the beach that had become a cold case for decades until it was resolved not long ago.

"I hear you," I sighed. "With 'no body and no blood,' as the officer told Max, I don't suppose they could have called Dave's disappearance a homicide even with the house in the shape it was in." I reached out to take Jack's hand.

Dave's amazing house of glass and steel, with its dramatic butterfly roof pointing skyward, could be seen from where we stood on the cliffs gazing down at the activity on the beach. A clifftop trail had led us from the maestro's estate to this spot. We'd passed through a gate from Dave's property onto a crudely worn path that was open to the public. Not only Malibu residents, but visitors used the trail to walk, jog, or gain access to the beach via a set of stairs. When we passed through it, Jack had stopped to examine the gate.

"The lock is operated by a keypad like the entry

MURDER OF THE MAESTRO

points into his house. Dave must have opened it unless someone else has the code. Pat has it, I'm sure, but she may not be the only one."

"The open gate must be the reason Pat insisted the police check the beach. Why would Dave have left it open?"

"Who knows? There's no sign anyone forced their way into his home. Any attempt to do that would have alerted Dave's security service. The intruder either had the code or Dave let the person in."

"If he knew the person he let into the house maybe they came out here for a stroll on the beach." Jack nodded, deep in thought. At one point, after we'd been walking in silence for a few minutes, I slid a little on the gravelly ground. Jack steadied me, but that wave of déjà vu I'd felt earlier was replaced by vertigo. I hadn't been in any real danger of falling, but if I'd been a little closer when I slid it might have been different.

"Do you think that's what happened to Dave— he lost his footing and fell? In the dark, if he got too close to the edge, he could have tripped or stumbled, before falling. The light of a full moon might not have been enough to help him see where he was going."

"It's possible. I'm sure he was more familiar with this path than we are, so it's hard to believe he fell because he lost track of where he was even in the low light."

"He'd been drinking at the gala. That could have made him unsteady on his feet or less aware of his surroundings." Suddenly my mind jumped the track and sped off in a different direction. "Of course, if he'd fallen and he was out here with a guest, why didn't his companion call for help immediately? Jack, what if he was running away from the intruder that trashed his house? In a panic, he could have lost track of where he was and then plunged off the cliff."

"It's too soon to rule anything out. If the maestro had too much to drink, that could explain why he forgot to shut the gate when he headed for the beach. Once we get the autopsy report, we'll know more about how much alcohol was in his system. There might also be something that tells us if he fell or was pushed."

"Dave was remarkably fit for a man in his seventies although I doubt he could have outrun a pursuer, especially one who was younger or more fit. Pushed is more likely, isn't it?"

"Yes, presuming he got this far on his own accord," Jack said, searching the path we were on and pointing to long indentions in the path. "The investigators snapped a few pictures of the path out here. They say there's no way to know how old these ruts are or what made them. Apparently, bikers use this path so that's probably where they came from. Still, it's not inconceivable someone hauled Dave out here and dumped him off the cliff."

"Like in a wheelbarrow or on a mover's dolly? Could one person have done that?" I asked.

"A wheelbarrow would have been hard to manage, but a wheeled cart of some kind, maybe. A mover's dolly is a pretty good alternative. Remind me not to tick you off and put you in touch with your inner cutthroat." Jack smiled wickedly as he said that.

"Oh, stop it!" Then I arched an eyebrow and donned a wicked little grin of my own. "You know I couldn't get you onto a mover's dolly by myself. Not unless I rigged up a pulley system to lift you or killed you on a bed and then rolled you off onto the dolly." Jack's mouth fell open.

"That's enough. You're starting to worry me, Doll," Jack said, adopting his hokey film noir detective voice. "I might have to hand you over to the cops for further questioning."

"Go right ahead. I'll happily tell them where I was last night until the wee hours of the morning. That would put you in a compromising situation, wouldn't it, Detective?" Jack threw back his head and laughed.

"An alibi's an alibi!" He took my hand and tugged me back down the path through the back gate that led onto Dave Rollins' estate. The walk was an easy one and hadn't taken long at all. The idea that someone had dragged or even rolled a body such a distance seemed more far-fetched, though, as I tried to imagine carrying out such a desperate maneuver by moonlight. As we walked across the lawn on Dave's estate, another possibility came to mind.

"So how about this? Dave's out for a romantic stroll with his lovely companion when things take a dark turn. Moonlight and romance become the setting for a lovers' quarrel that turns deadly. That would explain why his woman friend didn't report his fall."

"Something like that occurred to me, too," Jack said. "The rose left on the counter in the kitchen sure suggests romance was in the offing—or so Dave Rollins believed. Just because he had romance on his mind, didn't mean his guest did as well. Given the way in which his house looks, whoever dropped by for a visit must have had an entirely different mission in mind."

"Pushing him off the cliff first would have made it easier to search the house without worrying about Dave getting in the way or calling the police. But then why not make Dave hand it over rather than tearing the house apart to find it? What could he have had that was worth killing him to get it?"

"Great questions. Let's go see if your friend, Pat, is in any shape to tell us what's missing. That might help us answer your questions."

"Even if she can't tell us what's missing, she might tell us what the sneak thief rummaged through before taking off," I suggested.

"In a big hurry given that the front door was barely closed, and all the lights were left on. It's odd that a vandal or thief in such a hurry stopped long enough to turn on the music," Jack added.

"Vandalizing the house and turning up the music loud enough to rile the neighbors was an angry thing to do. Maybe whatever the intruder hoped to find wasn't there and that triggered the decision not just to search the place, but to trash it and make all that noise."

"It could be. But what's a little vandalism by someone angry enough to murder the old gent and steal from him?" Jack asked as we walked onto the patio behind Dave's house.

Before venturing into the morning room just off the expansive ultra-modern kitchen, we stopped to check in with a uniformed officer posted nearby. The sun that had risen above the horizon was pouring into the house now, bouncing off shiny surfaces of polished marble and stainless steel. Food was strewn about, here and there, on those surfaces. Glass shards, too.

The intruder had slung food with abandon, smashing jars from the refrigerator. Glassware and plates were shoved from cupboards, leaving their doors open. Surely, this was an act of rage. Would Dave really have stashed something of value in his fridge?

When Pat saw me, she reached out her arms interrupting my ruminations about the mess. My heart ached as I rushed inside to comfort her where she sat at a table in the morning room. She'd been out of it when Jack and I arrived earlier. EMTs, already called to the house in case Dave Rollins had been injured, had given Pat something to settle her nerves.

Before we'd arrived, Pat had agreed to go with the police officers to identify a man's body found on the beach. She was halfway down the stairs leading from the cliffs to the seaside below when she'd taken one look and verified that Dave Rollins was the man on the rocks. A moment later, she'd come close to joining him. A quick-thinking police woman had snatched Pat by the collar and yanked her away from the stair-railing before she'd tumbled over it in a fit of dizziness.

"I'm sorry I flaked out on you," Pat said as I sat down beside her.

"Don't worry about me. We heard what happened. Finding Dave like that had to be a shock."

Coming in through the front door as Jack and I

had done earlier, I'd experienced a jolt, too. The white walls were marred by blood-red streaks. Max's words, "No blood. No body," had come back to me right away, followed by the realization that Dave's house smelled like a bar. The vandal had used red wine to make those streaks. Not just on the walls, but on the maestro's white carpet, furniture, and his lovely white baby grand piano.

"It was a disturbing sight, even though I knew it had to be Dave. A white-haired man in a red velvet jacket—who else could it be? He loved that ridiculous smoking jacket. Not that he smoked anymore. The old fool had convinced himself it gave him an air of sophistication or some nonsense like that. He never came right out and said it, but I'm sure he believed it gave him an edge when he was pursuing a new woman."

"Is that why he was wearing it?" I glanced up at Jack who was hovering nearby. "Was a woman here with him last night?"

"I assume so. The smoking jacket, a single red rose, and a bottle of champagne upstairs on the balcony outside the office adjoining his master suite. It's Dave's prelude to romance."

"This one must have had a late start given that the gala didn't end until ten," I commented.

"Yes, most likely he and his date met there. I'll tell you the same thing I've already told the police. No, I don't know who he was entertaining last night. I sensed he wasn't alone when he called me and asked me to drop by after lunch today. When I left the gala, a crowd of well-wishers had him surrounded saying their goodbyes. That group included several attractive and attentive women. It could have been one of them or another woman hanging back to avoid being noticed. Who knows?" Pat's hands shook as she sipped a cup of coffee.

"I kept Dave's calendar when it came to his professional life; scheduling events, keeping up with correspondence on his behalf, reminding him of meetings, and making sure he showed up when and where he was supposed to show up. As his Personal Assistant, I ran lots of mundane errands like picking up his dry cleaning and prescriptions, but I drew the line at any involvement in his love life. I learned that lesson the hard way."

"What does that mean?" I asked. Pat squirmed under my gaze.

3 A LITTLE NIGHT MUSIC

"Years ago, when there was still a Mrs. Maestro, she didn't like the amount of time I spent with her husband even though it was my job. One birthday Dave asked me to buy a gift for her. I picked out this lovely diamond bracelet. When I showed it to him, she walked in and became convinced he'd given it to me. Dave handed her the note that the jeweler had inserted with the bracelet that read 'To my beloved wife,' or something like that. It wasn't enough. I was never able to interact with Marla again without feeling she was about to snarl or hiss at me."

"I'll bet she didn't turn that bracelet down, did she?" I muttered, recalling my encounters with Dave's wife over the years.

"No, she did not!" Pat tried to smile.

"If it's any consolation, Pat, she never liked me much either."

"I'm sure any woman who worked with Dave was on her list of potential rivals. I can't blame her for being suspicious. An attractive man with money and notoriety, there were always women throwing themselves at his feet. He seemed unable to resist the temptation to take advantage of what his adoring fans offered. Of course, Dave was never one to wait for a woman to make the first move. He was a gifted musician, a talented composer, and diligent about his art and career. Too bad he wasn't as committed to his marriage and family." Pat shrugged as she took another sip of coffee.

"In my case, her suspicions were unfounded. Dave was flirtatious, but after the brouhaha over Marla, he must have decided not to risk becoming involved with women at work." Pat nodded as if she understood what I was talking about.

"Their romance raised more than a few eyebrows at The Cat Factory, as I recall. I take back what I said about his career. That was a major lapse in judgment that could have killed some careers," Pat sighed at whatever old memories our discussion had raised.

"I hadn't given much thought in years to the stress surrounding his marriage and divorce from Marla. His kids are grown, now. At the time, they took the tongue-wagging about their famous father to heart. They were gawky teens with braces when lots of kids are a little embarrassed by their parents anyway. Time heals all wounds, doesn't it?"

"Some, maybe, but not all," I replied in a pensive mood. "I didn't pay too much attention to Dave's break-up. There had been rumors about other women even when his kids were younger. It never occurred to me to consider how big an impact all the gossip must have had on them. Was Marla behind the leaks to the media about his affairs or were his women friends the kiss and tell types?"

"I'm not sure. I doubt Marla was intent on preserving his reputation by the time she filed for divorce. She was always high strung and never hesitated to vent her anger about Dave's failings. If she flew off the handle when there happened to be members of the public around, so be it." Pat shrugged. "It was worse at home. I learned to get out of her way when she was ticked off—before she started throwing things."

"Did she ever injure you or anyone else?"

"No. The walls and furniture took a beating, but not me or Dave and the kids as far as I know. The shouting and screaming was loud at times, but no one ever called the police. Occasionally, she was so out of control, I was tempted to call them. The thought of the kids having to witness the police questioning their mother or arresting her just seemed wrong. Maybe that was a mistake, but once they divorced and she moved out, the worst seemed to be over. There was a row or two about money after that. They'd both get on the phone to their lawyers and their surrogates would fight it out."

Jack didn't say anything, but I could tell he was listening intently. If I had to guess, Marla was now suspect number one. Wives and girlfriends—ex or not—are always at or near the top of the list when a man is murdered.

"Dave's fondness for beautiful women continued after his divorce. Whenever I ran into him at concerts or company-related events, there always seemed to be one waiting in the wings, so to speak." Pat nodded in agreement.

"Quite literally, at times. As he grew older, the women he chose didn't, or so it seemed to me. It bolstered his confidence to have a beautiful, young woman standing off stage or sitting in the front row at a concert or theater performance." Pat paused and took another sip of water before speaking again. "He was a complicated person."

"No wonder he and Max were such good friends. Max doesn't chase women in the same way but he's the epitome of complicated, isn't he?" Jack made that comment from where he'd been standing, leaning against a wall, as he listened to our conversation.

"That's the truth, isn't it?" A smile crossed Pat's face. "I often wondered how two of the biggest egos on the planet could fit into the same room at the same time. They respected each other on a deeper level, I suppose, even when they fought it out like a couple of spoiled children."

"Max's saving grace is that he recognizes talent when he sees it. And, he knows his reputation along with Marvelous Marley World's bottom line rests on the work done by talented people. In his own way, Max deeply admired and appreciated Dave on many levels," I said. That was kind of an understatement. I couldn't count the number of times Max had bragged about Marvelous Marley World's legendary maestro and his genius.

"You're right. Some narcissists can't do that," Pat added.

"Did the conflicts between Max and Dave ever become violent?" Pat and I both turned our heads in Jack's direction and stared at him with our mouths hanging open. "Come on, I've got to ask."

"I doubt I caught every dispute, but I witnessed several real doozies. They involved lots of yelling, foot-stomping, and door-slamming. Dave would hurl his conductor's baton or tear up a piece of sheet music he was working on. Not the real deal, mind you, but a worthless bit of paper with scribbling on it. It was quite dramatic although they left less damage in their wake than when Dave and Marla fought it out." Something about the squabbles between Dave and Max brought another smile to her face.

"Their behavior was more buffoonish than vicious. They once took it out onto the lawn and faced off like a couple of old-time pugilists—that's the term Max used at the time. 'Let's settle this disagreement once and for all—like men, with a good old-fashioned round of pugilism.' Dave said sure and ran outside with Max on his heels. They circled each other with their fists pummeling the air. Just when I became concerned they might punch each other, Dave laughed and challenged Max to a duel instead! I believe that involved trying to drink each other under the table." The image of the men squaring off on Dave's perfectly manicured lawn made me smile. It quickly brought me back to the present when I considered the possibility that a more sinister dispute had taken place out there.

"Would Dave's prelude to romance have involved a walk around the grounds and a moonlit stroll along the cliffs or on the beach?"

"Oh, yes. I'm certain that was often part of his modus operandi." Pat dropped her eyes, leading me to wonder if there was more to her assertion than eavesdropping or hearsay. I hesitated to pry with Jack scrutinizing her every word in full-blown detective mode. Jack did not.

"How certain?" Jack asked.

"Quite certain. This will all come out at some point, anyway," she said, sighing loudly and making eye contact with me. "Years ago, before I became his Personal Assistant and before he married Marla, I fell under the maestro's spell for a short time. He wasn't as famous as he is now, but he was handsome, talented, and ambitious. I wanted to become a singer and he encouraged me. One thing led to another. He was renting a tiny beach house back then, but already had much of his routine in place—a single red rose, a glass or two of chilled champagne, a walk on the beach, and then 'a little night music' as he called it. That involved a private serenade on his violin. It was terribly romantic and almost before I realized it, I was swept up in a scene played out many times since then. One leading man with many female co-stars," Pat shrugged and sighed once again.

"What happened?" I asked softly. I could tell by the way she clenched and unclenched her hands, reliving that part of her past with Dave Rollins was still distressing.

"What always happened with Dave. He moved on. I moved out."

"Weren't you angry?" Jack asked.

"Yes. I was more hurt than outraged. Forewarned is forearmed, as they say. I entered the relationship telling myself every step of the way that I was headed toward a dead end. He never made promises or hid the fact that he was seeing other women. For a short time, I deluded myself into believing he'd grow out of it, or he'd come to care enough about me not to chase after other women or give in when they chased him. When one of the women he'd been courting turned up at his cottage and moved into a guest room, I got the message. I packed up and left."

"That was heartless!" I cried before I could stop myself. If he'd pulled that stunt on other women, there must be a line a mile long waiting for a chance to get even. How would we ever find his killer?

"How did you end up working for him as a PA?" Jack asked with an almost incredulous tone in his voice.

"Heartless, is right. Like I said, though, he was always straight with me. Perhaps more honest than I was since I'm not sure how much of my initial interest in Dave was tied to my professional ambitions rather than romance. After a few years in Hollywood, I came to appreciate the fact that he wasn't a predator, and that his lack of fidelity was out in the open and above-board—at least, with me. When it became clear I wasn't going to have a career as a singer or actress, I bumped into him again. His career had taken off and he needed someone trustworthy to support him. The job as his Personal Assistant paid very well, too. His offer beat what I was earning reviewing scripts for an agent and waiting tables."

"That still must have been difficult." I wondered how many women in Pat's circumstances could have been so forgiving. I could imagine plenty of them wanting to hurt him back!

"I took that second spin on the merry-go-round with Dave Rollins with my eyes wide open. No more wishful thinking. No youthful delusions. I had no interest in a romance, although we became friends. A few years later, he married. As I said, his wife was wildly suspicious of every woman in his life, including me. I never asked her if Dave had told her about us." Pat paused for a moment, then looked from me to Jack, and back to me. "Marla once told me his troubles with women were going to get him killed someday, and claimed they almost did when he was young. At the time, I figured she was being overly dramatic. What if she was right?"

"We'll try to figure that out," Jack replied. "I take it Dave never discussed the old troubles with women that Marla raised?"

"No. You'd think if he'd experience anything that serious when he was young he would have learned his lesson and changed his behavior. As much heartache as he caused the women in his life, break-ups always took a toll on him, too." Pat teared up. "I once asked him why he didn't just try going it alone for a while. You know what he said?"

"I can't even imagine," I replied.

"'I find my own company distasteful.' Wasn't that an awful thing to say?" A tear slid down Pat's face as she uttered that last statement. There was a tone of doleful finality that signaled to me she was about done with the questions. Jack didn't pick up on that.

"Does anything about his trouble with women or anyone else in his life, for that matter, come to mind as a reason someone searched the place?"

"Money must not have been the motive since there was plenty to steal that could have been turned into quick cash. To me, the destruction seems more about rage." Pat glanced at me with a puzzled expression on her face as if responding to a question I hadn't asked. "I've known unhappy women in Dave's life who expressed themselves by dumping a drink on him or returning some gift in shreds. Marla, even at her worst, never caused this much damage."

"Was that rage directed at anything in particular?" I asked.

"There's stuff everywhere, so it's hard to tell. Trash cans were emptied, storage bins upended, cabinets and drawers searched, and the contents thrown around. A couple of Dave's collectible jazz records were smashed in the process of going through them—accidently or on purpose? I don't know. Whoever did that also tossed his notebooks and sheet music onto the ground and poured wine all over them." I must have reacted in a visible way to the idea of Dave's music and memorabilia being damaged or destroyed. Pat shook her head.

"Don't worry. I doubt anything of great value related to his career is in the mess. Maybe that's what this was about—hoping to destroy some treasure from his legacy. He keeps the original sheet music for his important works locked up. His Marvelous Marley World memorabilia, too, like his Oscar and other awards, vintage movie posters, concert programs and other things like that have all been moved into the company vaults. Dave donated boxes and boxes of material this past year to the Marvelous Marley World archive. Those items aren't just valuable like his vintage jazz records. They're priceless and most are irreplaceable."

"From what you're saying, at least some of the items had to do with his career and weren't strictly personal." Pat paused to think about what Jack had said before speaking again.

"Yes, that is what I'm saying, although I'm not sure how you separate the man from his music. The police haven't given me free reign to go through the place in a systematic way, so I don't know what all is missing or destroyed. I noticed one thing that's not where he usually kept it."

"Something important?" I asked. Pat nodded, yes, but shrugged a little too. "What?" I asked urging her to tell us.

"The drawer to his writing desk upstairs in his master suite caught my eye because it was open. That's where he kept his checkbook day-to-day. I mentioned it to Sgt. Bardot, but it could be in another drawer or under items tossed onto the floor. Why take his checkbook and leave his Rolex and the diamond stick pin he wore to the gala last night lying there?"

"Unless there's something in that checkbook someone wanted to see or to hide," I suggested.

"I don't deal with his finances if I don't have to, so I could have it all wrong."

"Who handles money matters?" I asked.

"His accountant, Jennifer Wainwright."

"I know who that is. I've met her, Jack. She works at the same firm as Max's accountant."

"That's how Dave found her. The police also asked me about next of kin and beneficiaries of Dave's estate. I stayed out of those matters too. I told them to ask Jennifer. If she doesn't have the answers, she can find out. I believe his Estate Attorney works at her firm, too." Pat's shoulders drooped, as if too exhausted to straighten them.

"I'm sorry you've had to be on the frontlines with all of this."

"That's nothing new." She shook her head. "And, it's not over. Max has asked me to organize a tribute in Dave's memory. Maybe Marla or his kids will object and ask to do it instead, but I have a feeling it'll fall to me. My last act as his PA will be to help bury him."

"Well, I'm sorry too about the burden placed on you," Jack added. "I wish I could say the police are done with you, but that's not true. You were about as close to Dave Rollins as anyone. When you get a chance, if you could jot down a list of names of the women with whom Dave had bad break-ups? Let's start with the unhappy women in his life as we try to figure out who may have had it in for him."

"I will. The police sergeant who's roaming around upstairs already asked me if he had any enemies. I don't remember anyone, male or female, threatening to kill him. I promised to think about it. I'll come up with as many of the women's names as I can and maybe a light will go on about one of them or a man in their lives will come to mind." Another sad, exhausted sigh escaped her lips. I couldn't stand it.

"Listen, I'll help you with the memorial service for Dave. Carol, my Executive Assistant, can help, too. We're both adept at dealing with the organizational challenges that might come up at

Marvelous Marley World, depending on what Max is asking you to do."

"If you can run interference for me with Max, that would be a big help. He's more tyrannical than Dave!"

"Sure," I said, although "sure" was never a word anyone could use with any real certainty when it came to "Mad" Max Marley. Narcissism was only the tip of the psychoneurotic iceberg that comprised his mercurial mind. "Let's meet for lunch early next week and we'll talk more about it. In the meantime, Jack and I will speak to Marla. We'll ask her what role, if any, she or Dave's kids want to have in planning the event. I bet you're right that they'll be more than happy to leave the tribute in your capable hands."

"If you can do that, it would be an enormous relief. I don't relish dealing with Marla any more than with Max."

"Jennifer's going to get a call, too," I added. Jack fixed his gaze on me. "She may have names of other people we don't want to overlook as we plan a Marvelous Marley World farewell for Dave." Jack suppressed a smirk. I wasn't fooling him one bit. I was as eager as he and the police were to find out if there was anything of interest in that missing checkbook and who stood to gain by Dave's death. Pat didn't catch any of the byplay between Jack and me. A note of relief registered in her voice as she spoke again.

"Thanks, Georgie. That's great, too. I don't want to hurt anyone's feelings or step on toes, but I would like to get this done quickly. Lunch on Monday or Tuesday should be fine. Maybe by then I can tell you more about what's been stolen or destroyed around here. Odd, isn't it, to be planning another tribute to the maestro so soon after last night's retirement gala? That's life, I guess."

"I was thinking almost the same thing." *That's Life*, an old song made famous by Frank Sinatra, ran through my mind as she uttered those words. Written about the ups and downs faced by entertainers, it resonated with the sudden change of fortunes Dave had experienced in the past twenty-four hours. Up one day and down the next is the natural order of business in the fickle fields of art, theater, and music.

For Dave Rollins, though, there would be no comeback. Had his prelude to romance turned out to be a prelude to murder instead? Was the recipient of that red rose the one who killed him or had someone else orchestrated the sad finale to the maestro's life? I wondered if Jack was as curious as I was about the comments Pat claimed Marla had made about the maestro's troubles with women in his youth. It was hard to imagine anyone hanging onto revenge for decades, but maybe the key to his murder was in a secret from his past.

4 THE GOOD AGENT

As Jack and I said our goodbyes to Pat, we heard the doorbell ring. Raised voices followed. Jack didn't hesitate to go toward what sounded like an altercation. I could have hung back, but I had to know what was going on, too, so I dashed after Jack to the front door. A young uniformed police officer, with a weary expression on his face and a Lost Hills logo on his shirt, was blocking the way of a well-dressed man.

"I'm going to say it again. This is a crime scene. You can't come in here," the officer said, holding his arms out wide to prevent the man from gaining more ground on the inches he'd claimed of the stunning foyer. I recognized the bespectacled man with salt and pepper hair and a cleft in his chin.

"What kind of a crime scene?" He asked, trying to peer around the officer into the house. "I'm Dave's agent. Where is he? I heard there was trouble. People are depending on me to tell them what's going on." He took a step forward. Or tried to. The officer did not give ground. They were eyeball to eyeball. Then Bernie Morse glanced up and spotted me. "What's she doing here? I have as much right to be here as she does! Georgie, tell him who I am!" That command was issued in an imperious manner.

"Sorry, Bernie, I'm not in management around here. You need to do as the officer says." The beleaguered officer straightened his shoulders and stood a little taller.

I'm sure I sounded annoyed because that's how I felt. Who did Bernie think he was? One of my least favorite aspects of working with people in the entertainment industry is a *"Do you know who I am?"* sense of entitlement some adopt. Maybe after a year with a detective in my life, I'd also learned a little about how hard it is to figure out what's gone on at a crime scene even without uninvited people traipsing through it.

Bernie wasn't done yet. Instead of yielding, he stepped to one side as if preparing to barge in past the officer. Jack must have decided he'd had enough. Jack stepped forward and stood next to the uniformed officer who must have felt emboldened now that he had backup.

"I don't care who you are, you can't come in here without permission of the lead investigator, Sgt. Bardot. He's busy upstairs, so you'll just have to wait."

"Let's step outside, Bernie, and sort this out, okay?" Jack asked, motioning for me to follow as he flashed his badge at Bernie. The agitated agent shifted from one foot to the other. A jumble of papers he was carrying slid in his arms. He struggled to reorder them and dropped what looked like a checkbook. I glimpsed the initials on it as Bernie made a move to retrieve it.

"You'd better leave that right where it is," I said.

"Who suddenly put you in charge? You're not in management around here, remember?"

"Pat!" I hollered, rushing toward the kitchen. Pat came running and hustled after me when I did an about-face and headed back to the front door.

"What is it?" She asked as we reached the foyer.

"That's what I hope you can tell us. That wouldn't happen to be Dave's missing checkbook, would it?" Pat leaned over and examined the object on the floor.

"It sure looks like it. Most checkbooks are pretty much the same, but Dave had his monogrammed. See?" She pointed to gold letters I'd seen in one corner of the checkbook.

"What are you doing with Dave's checkbook?" I asked. Bernie gritted his teeth and grew antsy again, shuffling from one foot to the other. Then his shoulders slumped, and he stopped two-stepping. "I'm just trying to be a good agent for my client."

Yeah, right. The jig is up, I thought, wondering what sort of song and dance he was cooking up as Jack took charge.

"You're going to get your wish after all, Mr. Morse. Come on in and have a seat in the kitchen. I think we'd all be interested in hearing what you have to say in response to Georgie's question." Jack took Bernie by the arm and the two of them moved through the foyer and the great room, into the kitchen.

"Tony," Jack said addressing the Lost Hills police officer who now had a name. "While I escort Dave's good agent to the kitchen, will you please close and lock the door and then go upstairs and tell Sgt. Bardot a very important visitor has joined us?" Tony hopped to it, shut and locked the door, and then ran up the sweeping stairway to the floor above. Pat and I tagged along as Bernie shuffled as if Jack not only gripped his arm but had placed him in leg irons. His eyes widened as he caught sight of the disarray in the great room and the kitchen.

Jack seated Bernie at the same table in the morning room where Pat and I sat earlier. Sgt. Bardot came barreling into the room with Tony on his heels. When the senior officer stopped abruptly, Tony came close to bumping into him. That didn't go unnoticed by the sergeant.

"Will you get back out there to the front door and make sure we don't get any other unwelcome guests?"

"Sure," Tony replied, moving away at a snail's pace. I'm sure he wanted to hear Bernie's explanation for why he had that checkbook. Still within earshot of the conversation, Tony came to a halt, hovering in the background waiting for the action to continue.

"So, what gives? What are you doing with a dead man's checkbook?" Sgt. Bardot asked, taking the lead as you might expect him to do. Bernie's head snapped up from where he'd been staring at his fingernails. His face paled.

"Dead? Dave's dead?" Bernie asked as a tinge of green joined the pall left behind when the blood must have rushed from his head. "How? When? I just saw him last night at the gala and he was fit as a fiddle—in his glory!"

"How and when are questions we want you to answer since we believe someone took that checkbook from a desk upstairs during a break-in or a fight of some kind with Mr. Rollins. When and how did it happen to come into your possession?"

"He gave it to me." By the way Bernie was squirming, I found that hard to believe. The man had started to sweat too.

"When?" Jack asked.

"A couple of days ago."

"Really? Then, how come there's a check receipt in here with yesterday's date on it." Jack had donned latex gloves and held the checkbook open.

"Lying to the police isn't a good idea, is it Detective Wheeler?" Sgt. Bardot asked, smirking at Jack.

"Not during a murder investigation, that's for sure, Sgt. Bardot."

Hmm, I thought, *isn't one of them supposed to be the good cop?*

"M-m-murder! Marla couldn't have killed him. She told me Dave was still at that gala when she drove over here and picked up her check. It was hers, so why not?" Bernie shook his head and murmured to himself as though lost in thought, "Murdered…" Then he snapped to! "Are you saying she killed him? That conniving… she set me up!"

"If she came by to pick up her check, why take the checkbook, too?" I asked.

"She told me she took it to get back at Dave for

not bringing her check to the gala like he promised. Marla wanted to teach him a lesson by making him hunt around for it for a day or two—inconvenience him the way he'd done to her."

"Okay, maybe you should tell us again why *you* have it," Pat suggested.

"One of her old neighbors called us—er—her this morning to say there were cops in front of the house. Marla panicked, thinking he'd reported the checkbook as stolen. I said I'd take it back and drop it somewhere as if it had been there all along."

"Does that mean you spent the night with your client's ex-wife?" Jack asked.

"Yes. I didn't know she was planning to kill my client and use me as the dupe, like that sap in *Body Heat*." Bernie was clearly feeling sorry for himself, but he was more louse than sap in my book. As if we needed more of a demonstration that he was, indeed, a louse, he spoke again. "Marla's no Kathleen Turner, so definitely not worth this much trouble."

"And, you're no William Hurt," I groused. Bernie glared at me. Jack stifled a grin. "What time did you get to Marla's house?" I asked.

"It was nearly eleven."

"Pat, what time did Dave call you?"

"Late. I was in bed, exhausted by all the running around that went on even before that gala that lasted much later than planned. Hang on, and I can tell you the precise time." Pat dug through her purse she'd left on a counter in the kitchen. She pulled out her cell phone and scrolled through the calls.

"Eleven-forty-three." She shook her head as she gave the detectives that information. "I would have chewed him out today for calling me that late without giving me a good reason. Setting up a meeting, even at the last minute, could have waited until today." Pat sucked in a gulp of air, realizing how wrong that statement was under the circumstances. "Sorry to speak ill of the dead. Dead men don't make meetings, do they?"

I reached out and clasped her arm, hoping to console the woman who suddenly seemed less steady on her feet. I spotted a few bottles of water sitting in a tray on the edge of the kitchen island and handed her one. Coffee made, and beverages set out—the woman had been at the house for hours and must have gone into hostess mode at some point.

Dead men still have Personal Assistants, I mused to myself as Jack spoke.

"If Bernie's telling us the truth, Dave was still alive after he arrived at Marla's house." I suppressed my disappointment that Bernie probably wasn't going to get arrested for murdering Dave Rollins. For now, I couldn't think of a nicer end to this episode than watching Tony haul Bernie off to spend the night in jail.

"What about it, Bernie? Are you telling us the truth?" Sgt. Bardot asked.

"Call Marla. She'll tell you what time I got to her house."

"So now you want us to believe the woman who set you up for murder is going to provide you with an alibi?" Bernie thought about Jack's question for a few seconds.

"You call her, or I will! I also believe I'm entitled to call my lawyer," Bernie replied. "In fact, I'm not

39

saying another word until he gets here."

Despite claiming he wasn't going to say another word, more conversation followed. I didn't hear it because my phone rang. I scrambled to dig out the phone as that ringtone blasted out the melody Dave had written so many years ago. It made me sad to hear the jaunty notes. What made me even sadder was the identity of the caller.

"Max," I said and then paused to take a deep breath. Jack and Pat spoke almost in unison.

"You'd better talk to him."

"Yeah, I know, but what am I going to say?" I walked away from the group gathered around Bernie. The good agent struck me as a ticking time bomb likely to explode at any moment with outrage. I stepped out onto Dave Rollins' expansive patio overlooking the Pacific Ocean and gulped sea air.

"Max, how are you doing? I'm afraid I don't have much news for you since Pat called to tell you about Dave's death. I'm so sorry." An unearthly silence followed. Max, speechless, is a rare event. That he didn't interrupt me as I explained what we'd learned since arriving at Dave's home was unprecedented. When he did speak, his voice was weary, but determined. Max Marley has a will of iron.

"So, what are you doing next?" He asked. I wasn't quite sure what to say when Jack appeared at my side.

"Come on," Jack said.

"Hold on. Maybe I can tell you what's next," I told Max. I clamped a hand over the cell phone in case I didn't want Max to hear what Jack had to say.

"We're going to go interview a person of interest

for Sgt. Bardot," Jack replied. "You know her far better than I do, so I'm taking you with me."

"Uh, Jack tells me we're going to interview someone for the police," I didn't explain further, and Max didn't ask for more information.

"Go, go, go! Keep me posted, though. Call me immediately if you find out who did this monstrous thing to Dave. In the meantime, I trying to figure out how to handle this with our Associates and the public. It's a difficult loss for the Marvelous Marley World family. Monstrous, just monstrous," Max muttered to himself as he ended the call.

As self-proclaimed head of the family, "Uncle Max," was obviously trying to come to grips with the situation. Not just for business reasons, either, as the anger and sadness in his voice revealed. The demand that we keep him informed was delivered more as a plea than an order.

"Poor Max," I said as I hustled after Jack to our car parked out in front of the maestro's house. Right now, the entrance gate at the street was open. It wouldn't have been that way Friday night. "This is the only entrance from the street, right?" I asked Jack moments later as we drove through it.

"Yep. The only other way to get onto the property is through the back gate."

"It had to be someone close to him, then," I muttered.

"Like an ex-wife, you mean?" I nodded in response. A knot formed in my stomach at the thought of facing Marla under the circumstances. On a good day, she was hard to take. This wasn't a good day by any stretch of the imagination.

"Buckle up, Detective. If I know Marla, it's going to be a bumpy ride."

"Yes, you do know Marla and I'm hoping if I miss something, you'll catch it. By bumpy, do you mean she's going to be on a crying jag playing the grieving widow, even though she and Dave are no longer married?"

"No. Not unless there are cameras around. She's quite good at striking a pose or putting on a show like that for the media. In private, we're more likely to get a glimpse of the Marla Broussard Pat had to deal with so often. I've caught her in action a time or two. Our catering associates have had run-ins with her in tantrum-throwing, diva mode many times. She's not shy about expressing her dislike for a dish by hurling it."

"At someone?"

"I'm not sure that was the intention, but she's come close to it."

"Maybe Dave Rollins was lucky he lived as long as he did." Jack stared at me. "None of what Pat had to say about her must have come as a surprise to you."

"Not a bit of it."

"She'd better hope her alibi holds up."

5 THE EX-MRS. MAESTRO

"Yes, I was at his house. So, what? Is it my fault the fool fell off the cliffs?" As I'd expected, Marla was anything *but* grief stricken. She was suspicious from the moment we arrived and I introduced her to Jack. Then she grew indignant as soon as he asked her a few basic police detective questions.

"Who said that's how he died?" Jack asked.

"Are you kidding? Someone gave him a push?" Marla Broussard asked and then paused. Jack said nothing in reply to her questions. Then she looked at me as if searching for confirmation. I shrugged slightly, trying to remain noncommittal since we really didn't know for certain how Dave had ended up at the bottom of the cliffs.

"What Jack's asking is how you knew he didn't just die in his bed from a heart attack."

"His neighbor called me and said he'd fallen to his death. Dying in bed from a heart attack would have served him right, the old coot. A dive off the cliffs is a much more dramatic end for the maestro though, isn't it? Especially if someone pushed him. Now that's a story!" Jack still said nothing, but he raised his eyebrows.

"Don't look at me like that, Detective. Dave wasn't even home yet when I got to his place. Besides, I was wearing a pair of heels almost exactly like these. They're great for man-chasing, but not in a literal sense, if you know what I mean?" She batted her eyelashes at Jack, and then sighed in an exasperated way as he fixed her with a withering gaze.

"Oh, come on. Even he could have outrun me while I was wearing shoes like these," as she said that, Marla stretched, turning her ankle for Jack to get a better look at those shoes and her legs. "That's especially true if he got anywhere near those stairs before he took that dive. I hated walking down those stairs to the beach even when I wasn't in spiky heels." Jack's eyes narrowed as he deployed his worldly-wise, detective's truth-o-meter, measuring the "ex-Mrs. Maestro" as she sat across from us.

"Why would I kill him? He's my meal ticket—or would have been for a while longer. Shoving the golden goose off a cliff would have been stupid. At least, until my current prospect pops the question."

That must have done something to Jack's assessment of the woman because he blinked and shifted in his seat. Her analysis was shamelessly self-serving, but her logic was brutally frank.

She and Bernie are made for each other, I thought, remembering how quickly Bernie Morse had concluded that the lovely Marla Broussard had set him up for murder.

"Would that be your dead ex-husband's agent?" I asked.

"Maybe. What's it to you? I don't even understand why I'm speaking to either of you without my lawyer present."

Another totally self-serving comment. It came as no surprise to me that Marla Broussard was a piece of work. I'd mingled with her on occasion after she married Dave, but she worked at Marvelous Marley World before she married her way up and out of The Cat Factory. Younger than Dave Rollins by many years, their affair had been considered scandalous, especially when their daughter was born six months after a hasty marriage in Reno.

I was a little surprised by her willingness to speak to us, but if she and Bernie were serious enough to be considering marriage that would explain it. Bernie had asked her to do it. After consulting his lawyer, Bernie had called Marla and explained that Jack and I would be right over. When she asked why, he didn't say a word about corroborating his alibi, but stuck with the script he'd been given.

"They have some questions for you about Dave and they want to clear up confusion about why I'm at his house this morning. I told them you could do that."

Here we were, face-to-face with her, in a swanky home in Pacific Palisades. I scanned the well-appointed room around me and could believe that Marla didn't want to give this up.

"I've confirmed what Bernie told you. I was in my ex-husband's house last night while the maestro was still being heralded as a genius. So, what?"

"How did you get in?" Marla tapped one of her stiletto-shorn feet.

"I used to live there, Georgie. Remember? I still have the code. He changed the entry code on the security system from time-to-time, but he'd give me the new one. Or he'd give it to the kids and they'd give it to me. They've both stayed in the guest wing of his house if they wanted to spend a weekend at the beach—sometimes even while he was away doing concerts and recitals."

Dave and I were colleagues at Marvelous Marley World the entire time I'd worked there, although he'd been hired years before me. It wasn't until I moved into management that I ran into him much. Even then, we weren't close associates. My role in Food and Beverage Management sometimes crossed over into the entertainment side of Marvelous Marley World Enterprises. That usually happened when our caterers provided services during rehearsals and business meetings or for opening night concerts, theater, or film premiers.

When Dave and I chatted at one of those galas, he sometimes mentioned Marla or one of his children. I had no idea he saw them on what sounded like a regular basis. The last I heard, his daughter, Katie, was in San Francisco and his son, Carter, was in San Jose. Katie was musical, Carter was not, if I remembered correctly.

"This is really no big deal. I knew where Dave kept my check. I picked it up and left."

"What about the checkbook? Bernie says you took it to get back at your ex-husband?" I asked.

"That's where Bernie's winging it, or he

misunderstood me. I didn't take it on purpose. What I told Bernie is that I had *considered* taking it on purpose to hassle Dave since he'd 'forgotten' to bring my check with him to the gala as he'd promised. I'll be honest and tell you that the idea crossed my mind, but I put it back, or so I thought. When I realized Dave was expecting company, I was in such a rush to get out of there, I took off with it."

"Why were you in that big a hurry if the gala wasn't even over yet?"

"I thought I heard a car pull up. The last thing I wanted to do was run into Dave with some young thing on his arm, while he was still basking in the glory of being the maestro." To me, it was entirely possible for Marla to be as shallow and banal as her explanation appeared to be, but Jack's face registered skepticism.

"If you're looking for a confession, here's one. I was tempted to jerk Dave around by dropping the checkbook into the trash can next to his desk or tossing it off his balcony and into the ocean. After all, he could have made life easier for me if he'd set up an automatic payment to my account. Instead, I had to contact him every month, like a beggar asking for a handout instead of getting what I was owed after putting up with his massive ego and roving eye. Even at home that mousy PA was always underfoot. Why would he set Pat up with an office in our home unless some sort of hanky-panky was going on?" Marla was getting worked up. The knot in my stomach was back. Fortunately, Jack switched the subject.

"I take it if Dave's place had been turned upside down when you arrived you would have called the police, right?" Jack didn't even blink as he asked that question.

"Turned upside down? Are you serious?" She appeared to be genuinely puzzled. Dave's neighbor who called to tell Marla he'd fallen off a cliff must not have known about that part. When neither of us jumped in with a response, Marla continued speaking. "Only an idiot would go into her ex-husband's house if it had been trashed. I'm no idiot. The place looked perfectly normal. Normal for Dave in Casanova mode, anyway, with his little mousetrap all set to snag some starry-eyed wannabe 'it girl.' I spotted the rose, his smoking jacket on the valet stand, the empty ice bucket waiting to be filled, and the little bauble lying there like a bit of cheese to lure the mouse into the trap."

"A bauble—what kind of a bauble?" I asked. Jack went on alert.

"A diamond-studded, treble-clef shaped pin. Not very original, is it? He must have bought them in bulk, too, since his date last night would have been only one of many to wear the maestro's pin."

"Where was it?" Jack had pulled his phone out of a pocket. I presume he intended to send a text message to Sgt. Bardot who was still at the house when we left.

"On his writing desk in his office off the master suite. Right next to a single red rose." Marla shifted in her seat, and one foot tapped the floor. Jack and I glanced at each other.

"What? I didn't take it—I already have one. If it's gone, Dave must have reached the gift-giving stage of the evening." Before we left to interview Marla, Jack and I had taken a quick look around upstairs. Sgt. Bardot had shown us the open drawer in the desk where the checkbook was usually kept. No rose—we'd seen it on the kitchen island. No diamond pin, either, unless it was among items on the floor. I could picture Sgt. Bardot or Tony searching for it.

"Does that happen before or after the romantic moonlit stroll?" Marla's eyes narrowed as she stared at me with renewed suspicion. If she mistakenly believed I had personal knowledge of what she'd referred to as Dave Rollins' Casanova mode, I intended to correct her right away. "Pat already gave us the rundown on his routine," I offered. Marla's mouth twisted into a grimace.

"Of course, she did. Pat's probably seen him in action more times than me. The presentation of the rose comes first. Then he pours a round of champagne from a bottle in the kitchen, suggests a stroll, and promises a tour of the house when they return. That tour ends up on the balcony outside his master suite where more champagne awaits. If he's really trying hard to impress, he might throw in a private violin performance. Find that little mouse who was with him last night and I bet she'll have that diamond pin."

"When you left the house, did you see a car—the one you heard pull up?" Jack asked.

"No, thank goodness. No car. No people. I got all the way home before I realized I had Dave's checkbook. Since I figured he was going to be busy all evening, I planned to call Dave today and tell him I had it."

"So, what was Bernie doing with it?"

"This morning when a neighbor called and said there was big trouble at Dave's house, Bernie and I both became concerned about what it might look like if the police found out that I had the stupid checkbook with me. It was Bernie's idea to talk his way inside and drop it somewhere as if Dave had mislaid it."

"Wouldn't it have been smarter to pass it along through your lawyer, along with a statement about how it came to be in your possession?" I wasn't quite sure that was true, but it made more sense than the scene Bernie had made by showing up and bullying a young police officer to get inside and ditch that checkbook as he'd planned. Marla shrugged.

"Okay, so Bernie's not the genius he thinks he is. That doesn't mean either one of us had anything to do with Dave's death. Maybe this time, his starlet wannabe turned out to be a cute young thing hankering for a role in a *Fatal Attraction* movie. Or maybe he picked one with a psycho husband or some other man in her life who objected to her sneaking around with the high and mighty maestro. It wouldn't be the first time Dave's womanizing got him into trouble." Marla folded her arms and crossed her legs. To me, both actions signaled she was trying to contain herself as she grew more agitated.

"What does that mean?" Jack asked.

"Please, Detective, you're not that naïve, are you? He wooed them, won them, and then ditched them. Can you possibly imagine that didn't cost him a pretty penny now and then even without an angry spouse in the picture? Dave's troubles with women started a long time ago, according to my cousin, Yvonne. I don't know the details, but she told me I'd married the black sheep in a family that had disowned him because of a youthful indiscretion with the wrong woman. It would have been nice of Yvonne to have warned me off, but old southern families are pretty closed-mouth about scandal. It wasn't until I told her I'd filed for divorce, she let me in on that little tidbit. Even then she was evasive about it. I didn't care enough about Dave by then to pursue it."

I found that impossible to believe. Having a juicy secret from his past to hang over her ex-husband's head would have given her leverage. Surely enough to get him to agree to automatically deposit those checks as she longed for him to do. Or it might have been worth a few bucks—either from Dave or one of the tabloids who thrive on exposing the dirty little secrets of the rich and famous. Unless there was nothing to it. Jack wasn't convinced either.

"You were married to Dave Rollins for years and you never wondered about his family ties—or the absence of them?"

"He told me he didn't have much family. I took his word for it that his brother Bill and Aunt Meg were it. Not that I had any involvement with them either. Heck, I don't have much to do with my family other than my kids. Yvonne was well off, but too many of my other relatives had dollar signs in their eyes when they came calling. I learned to put out the 'Do Not Disturb' sign soon after word got out that I'd married the maestro. I figured Dave's relatives were as greedy as mine and he'd learned to avoid them. I suppose one of them could have made him pay for not sharing the wealth. Or maybe his death is related to that black sheep business."

What was Marla up to? I wondered. Was she trying to cast suspicion elsewhere or did she really believe a dark secret in his past had caught up with Dave decades later?

"Does your cousin Yvonne share your last name?" I asked.

"Yes, but the only place you'll find it now is on her gravestone. Cousin Yvonne Broussard died two years ago."

"How about Dave's brother Bill or his Aunt Meg—do you know how we can find them?" Jack asked.

"I have no idea. I bet Pat knows how to reach them. It wouldn't surprise me if she knows all Dave's dirty little secrets. With her front row seat in his life, I don't see how she could have missed a bit of the trouble he had with women—old or new!"

"Can anyone else verify what time you arrived home last night or when Bernie joined you?"

"As a matter of fact, I was on the phone with Katie when Bernie arrived. Ask her. Other than that phone call, I don't have a selfie or anything to prove I was home in bed at the time. I'll bet you can ping me or use some trick like that to figure out exactly where I was when I made that call, can't you, Detective?"

I don't know about Jack, but I wished I had a trick or two to use on Marla Broussard. She'd gone back into flirty mode as she mentioned that selfie in bed thing. I tried to imagine any circumstance in which I'd rely on flirting to cope. It certainly wouldn't be one that involved an interview with a police detective about a murder investigation. Especially when the dead guy was an unfaithful ex-husband and the cop's wife was sitting right beside him! It was obvious to me that she was still jealous of Dave's involvement with other women even though their marriage had ended years before. *How jealous?* I wondered.

"Katie can vouch for Bernie, too, since I told her he'd arrived, and I had to get off the phone."

"What about your son? Where was he?"

"You must be joking! Are you insinuating that Dave's son killed him? Dave wasn't much of a husband, but he was a doting father." For the first time, Marla showed signs of sadness about Dave's death. "They doted on him, too. Carter was still at the gala last night when I left. He had a plane to catch later, so he left you an easy trail to follow. Katie and Carter are devastated, so if you have more questions, please have the decency to give them a day to deal with their father's death." Her voice sounded angry, but her eyes glistened with tears. "Don't you have any better suspects to pursue than my children or me?"

"Do you?" Jack asked.

"Follow the women is my recommendation. If there's a man out there with worse Karma than Dave when it comes to a faithless heart, I've never heard of him." Then she sighed. "I could use a little time to come to grips with Dave's death too if you two don't have any more questions."

"Well, when you and your children have had time to talk it over, Max has asked us to organize a memorial tribute for Dave. If you want to participate in the planning, you're more than welcome to do that. If not, it would be great if we could send you a summary of what we're proposing. Members of the

Marvelous Marley World family would appreciate having you, Katie, and Carter be part of the celebration somehow." Marla nodded.

"Sure. We can send you a batch of family photos. The kids and I will have to go through those anyway to put together a display during the visitation and funeral. Please don't make us go back to the same location where the retirement gala was held. I'd like to keep the memory of the two events separate." She stared at me. "Whatever you do will be top notch. Dave always appreciated that about you. What a jerk to get himself killed the moment he retires!"

Marla had run out of steam. What a puzzle she was when it came to Dave. It was almost as if there were two Marlas.

Which one's real? I wondered as Jack wrapped things up. He left his card and asked her to call if she remembered anything

"Do you believe her?" I asked Jack once we were in the car and on our way home.

"Not the bit about the missing checkbook. I think Bernie's story is probably closer to the truth. Marla Broussard strikes me as the kind of spiteful person who enjoyed making Dave Rollins miserable when she could. I do believe she didn't want to push him too far, since the golden goose was still subsidizing her lifestyle."

"Pushing him off a cliff would have been too far, I guess," I said, yawning as I spoke.

"Getting bored with this case already, huh?" Jack asked, stopping for a red light and grinning at me.

"Marla's a bore, that's for sure with that ridiculous flirting routine," I groused. "In addition to being spiteful, she's obviously still jealous after all these years. If that were a reason to kill him, she would have done it already."

"True. She seemed more annoyed than angry about his infidelity. Her flirting and the decision to hide Dave's checkbook, come across as manipulative and passive aggressive, but not furious enough to bash his brains in or destroy his house."

"Dave's brutal demise does feel more like the actions of a Glenn Close type—like in that *Fatal Attraction* movie Marla mentioned, doesn't it? Maybe Marla's onto something with her follow the women comment. Good luck with that," I harrumphed. Dave's foolishness didn't make any more sense to me than did Marla's. "If Marla's daughter backs her up, she's got a pretty good alibi, doesn't she?"

"Yes, she does. Marla's a living testament to the fact that old wounds don't always heal, though. Some fester and become more poisonous over time. Let me buy you a cup of coffee while I call and see what Sgt. Bardot wants to do about digging into the deep dark secrets in Dave Rollins' past." At the next stoplight, Jack turned into a shopping center not far from Crystal Cove State Beach. It sits below the hillside on which we live and is a place we visit regularly.

"That's a great idea. We can pick up takeout for lunch." I had a call to make too. Whatever Sgt. Bardot decided to do about Dave Rollins' past, an idea had popped into my weary brain already. My clever and resourceful Executive Assistant was about to earn herself another spa day. That's the bonus I give Carol whenever she does extra duties as a snoop. I could already see her hunched over in front of her computer with her fingers flying across the keyboard, searching for the maestro's secrets.

6 SIR JACK OF CRYSTAL COVE

Ah, what a difference a good night's sleep can make. When the alarm went off, I also heaved a sigh of relief that our day hadn't started with a bellowing cat, a zany ringtone, or a frantic phone call from Max. Or a murder.

Instead, Sunday rolled in like the languid waves Jack and I watched from our perch overlooking Crystal Cove State Beach. Traffic was light on the Pacific Coast Highway that runs alongside the coastline here in the OC. My veranda, where Jack and I sat sipping coffee and eating breakfast, is high enough up on the hillside opposite the cove that the ocean usually succeeds in masking the noise from commuters or beach goers.

This morning it was exceptionally quiet. The tranquility and beauty of the scene sat in jarring opposition to the ugly one we'd witnessed in Malibu yesterday. I almost dreaded asking, but I couldn't stop myself. The compulsion to find out who murdered the maestro was just too strong.

"Any updates from Sgt. Bardot or Pat?" I asked.

"The only news I have is that Pat's going back there today and pick through the debris now that the Lost Hills police and crime scene investigators have finished their work." As he responded, Jack picked up his phone and glanced at it. I presume he was making sure he hadn't missed a call or text. My dutiful husband is as compulsive as I am about getting to the bottom of disturbing situations.

"I hope she's in better shape today than she was yesterday. Are you sure it's safe for her to be there alone? Maybe an officer ought to accompany her."

"She's not going to be there alone. My new pal, Sgt. Hank Bardot, and I, who are now on a first name basis by the way, learned something else from her. Since you have more experience dealing with members of the rich and famous like the maestro, it's probably not news to you."

"What's that?"

"Personal Assistants have assistants."

"Hmm, I'm not sure if I knew that or not. That Dave had an entourage makes sense given the relentless pace he led. He was a busy man behind the scenes as Chief Creative Officer for the Marvelous Marley World Music Group. He loved being in the limelight, too, and often conducted the orchestras that performed his compositions or musical arrangements. Dave really hammed it up, playing the role of celebrity to the hilt in his stunning Marvelous Marley World outfits specially designed for him. I'll bet Dave had an assistant who did little other than care for his wardrobe."

"I spotted a couple of those photos hanging in

his home office where he was decked out in full period regalia as if he were Beethoven or Brahms. In another one, he was dressed in an even wilder looking costume like something Elton John might have chosen to play the part of an orchestra conductor."

"Elton John's a perfect comparison. Dave usually had several costume changes during a concert. Until a few years ago, he sometimes played a violin or piano solo during a show. Audiences expected him to take center stage in a getup they could see from any seat in the house."

"A true superstar, huh?" Jack asked.

"Yes, and with a superego to match, apparently. What on earth was he thinking by playing the field with so many women?"

"Maybe he figured if he kept at it long enough, he'd eventually get it right. It sounds like he believed that in love, like music, practice makes perfect."

"A perfect idiot if he imagined his stale, old Hugh Hefner routine was romantic," I huffed.

"He does seem to have dug a rut for himself. Then again, not every guy's as lucky as me. I made a mistake or two before I bumped into you and found the woman of my dreams. Things could have gone terribly wrong even then since we met at the scene of a murder that pointed to you as a wild-eyed slasher."

"Well, I'm lucky, too, since you helped me beat the rap, Copper. It wouldn't have worked out so well for either one of us if I'd been locked up for a murder. Thanks for the assist," I said leaning over to give my handsome husband a kiss.

"It was the only decent thing to do for a classy dame who saved me from a tragic future as a sad old

ANNA CELESTE BURKE

lonesome lothario like the maestro." I didn't say anything but, in my opinion, Jack would have to undergo a drastic personality change to become a lothario, lonesome or otherwise. He'd been unlucky in love the first time around and his marriage had ended in divorce. Until we met, he'd been almost as reluctant as I'd been to believe you get a second chance at love. Bad luck hadn't stopped Dave.

"If that luckless lothario had hung up his ruby red velvet smoking jacket years ago he might still be alive." Jack nodded.

"You could be right. The ex-Mrs. Maestro isn't the only woman with a reason to bear a serious grudge against Dave. What's your take on Pat's story about being one of the maestro's many 'exes'?"

"It's obvious to me she still has—or had— feelings for him. I believe she's being truthful when she says she'd come to grips with the fact that he was troubled when it came to women. Still, it occurs to me that if Dave had ever come to his senses, the woman of his dreams was already at his side. I'm pretty sure she would have given him a second chance if he'd asked for it in a serious way."

"Perceptive, as always. My sentiments run along the same lines, although I doubt I could have stated them as articulately as you just did."

"Be that as it may, Pat seems to have settled for what she could have with him. She's no scorned woman. In fact, she was probably the woman in his life with whom he had the longest, closest relationship. Did you hear who was going to be with her today at Dave's house?"

"Yes. Adam Middlemarch is the assistant she's

60

taking with her. I'll add him to the list of people we should check out. He's been around for years, though. If he's the one who wanted to do away with Dave, he's had ample opportunity to do it."

"Unless he's had a recent beef with the maestro," I muttered trying to recall what I knew about Adam Middlemarch. "As far as I can tell, he's a cross between an errand boy and a handyman. He's a big guy pushing thirty, so he could easily have overcome Dave and shoved him off the cliff. Adam appears to be a quiet, unassuming man, although I've only run into him a few times. It's hard to picture him as an angry killer or destroying the house he'd helped keep in tip-top shape for years."

"I often have more trouble taking the measure of a quiet man than a boisterous one like Max. As a handyman he would have had an access code to get through the gates and into the house without breaking in. Who knows what lurks beneath that silence?" Jack looked a little worried. That gave me the shivers.

"That's a good question for Pat, isn't it?"

"Maybe not in those exact words. I'll ask her if Adam and the maestro have had a "beef" as you so eloquently put it—recently or not."

"You may have less experience with the rich and famous, but you've been around many more suspicious characters than I have so you'll be a better judge of Adam than me. If he's more of a raging bull than the strong, silent type maybe Pat's not safe with him."

"This can't be the first time she's been alone with him. Besides, an insurance adjuster is also supposed to meet them there to assess the damage. Working for Marvelous Marley World must give you clout even from the grave to get an insurance company to send an agent out there fast, and on a Sunday to boot!"

"With a property like Dave's, the insurers know the best way to cut their losses is to clean and repair the place as soon as possible. I'll bet Max is the one pulling the strings to get that kind of service rather than my dead colleague. You're going to get to the bottom of this soon, aren't you? I don't like the idea that a killer's still on the loose or that Max is lurking in the background ready to pull our strings like some crazed puppet-master if he loses it. When I told him Dave was dead, it was clear to me he was fighting for control. He won't be able to contain himself for long."

"I understand what you're saying, but not even Max can rush justice." I put my fork down when my stomach twisted as if Max had just overheard Jack utter those words. My eyes roamed the beach off in the distance where a few people were ambling along, enjoying a leisurely Sunday stroll. Jack and I planned to do that next to get in a bit of exercise and to unwind from the stressful events in which we'd become embroiled. I was suddenly inspired to suggest an alternative.

"How about we take our Sunday stroll along the beach in Malibu today? I'll call Pat and tell her we're stopping by and you can meet the assistant's assistant for yourself."

"That's a great idea. I'd like to get a better look at how someone can get to Dave's estate by starting from the beach and working our way up to the house.

Put your criminal mind to work too, will you? Help me identify spots where a person might have hidden until the maestro showed up during his moonlit walk, with or without a companion."

"My criminal mind? What are you saying?" Even as I asked that question, I was running over the path we'd trod, wondering where I might have concealed myself if I'd wanted to catch Dave by surprise. "Once a suspect, always a suspect," I mumbled as I continued trying to recall every inch of that trail we'd walked. Jack laughed.

"Let's go!" He said as he stood and picked up his coffee cup and breakfast dishes. I cleared the remaining items from our table and dashed after him from the veranda to the kitchen sink.

"It's much better to stay on the right side of the law, don't you think? I wouldn't want the two of us on the case if I were the culprit who killed Dave." I put my dishes into the dishwasher as Jack had just done with his. Jack laughed again, and this time pulled me close to him for an embrace that made me quite happy we'd met even if it had been at an awful crime scene.

"I'm glad I didn't have to break any laws to get you on my case! I'm not sure I could resist the temptation to become an outlaw if that's what it took." It was my turn to laugh. Jack as an outlaw was as fanciful as his notion he might someday have ended up as a lonesome lothario.

"Oh, come on. You don't fool me. You're a Boy Scout and you know it! Let's go rescue a damsel in distress," I said and gave him the little three-finger scout salute.

"I'm pretty sure that rescuing a damsel in distress qualifies me to be your knight in shining armor." Jack had this wickedly handsome grin on his face that reminded me so much of James Garner in The Rockford Files. Maybe it was the fact that we were headed to Malibu where that series was filmed that had brought the character to mind. I gave Jack a smooch.

"Okay, have it your way, Sir Jack of Crystal Cove. Let's go. I'm calling Pat to tell her we're on our way whether she needs rescuing or not." A bellow from Miles signaled disapproval. "What's your problem, cat? You don't go to the beach—here or in Malibu. Nobody's leaving you out of anything." When Miles tilted his head back and roared again, I got the shivers. Jack must have seen my reaction.

"It's okay, Miles. I won't let a sea monster or dragon get anywhere near our lady fair. That's why she's taking Sir Jack along." I doubt Jack meant it the way it sounded, but it struck me as funny. That proclamation issued with such bravado sent the heebie-jeebies fleeing.

"Hmm, okay, Sir Jack-along. I don't know about Miles, but I'm convinced."

"I much prefer Sir Jack of Crystal Cove," Jack said, bowing low. "Shall we go?"

I grabbed the windbreakers we wear to the beach and pulled my phone from a shoulder bag and called Pat. She picked up on the second ring. It occurred to me later that making that phone call had not been such a good idea.

7 A SUNDAY STROLL

Less than an hour later we were strolling along the nearly empty beach in Malibu. The Pacific Ocean is frigid this time of year. Even though it was sunny, the air was chilly. A few hardy souls sat on the beach to read or gaze at the horizon, but no one was in the water. A jogger ran out ahead of us, and a dog barked as he chased a gull into the water, setting the bird to flight. Otherwise, it was quiet except for the sound of lazy waves rolling onto shore.

As we did a few stretches, I felt uneasy. Maybe it had been the edgy tone in Pat's voice. When I'd spoken to her, it was clear she had plenty of company for the time being. The insurance adjuster had arrived, not alone but with an entire team. Maybe more of Max Marley's handiwork. She and Adam had started showing them around and had just begun to assess the damage on the first floor.

Since she was busy, we'd opted to make our way to Dave's house via the beach route Jack wanted to examine. We set out at a pace that could pass as exercise until we approached the spot where Dave's body had been found. As we drew closer, I became more apprehensive. Why not? Our *Sunday stroll* was, after all, leading us to the scene of a murder.

Fortunately for me, when we arrived a half hour later, I discovered that wind and water had left no trace that a crime of any kind had taken place. The police and forensic team had cleaned up after themselves leaving no photo markers or tape or any other remnants of their investigation behind.

"Why not wait for the maestro down here to kill him? There are plenty of places to hide," I wondered aloud.

"Maybe the killer didn't want to get wet or didn't want to get sand in the car on the way home," Jack quipped. Then he spoke again in a more somber tone. "It's more likely that whoever murdered Dave felt he or she was less easily observed up there on the bluff above the beach."

"I guess that could be true. If you have murder on your mind, the clifftop trail might seem less public—even at the late hour and in the dark when the beach must have been emptier than it is now." I headed toward the foot of the stairs that would take us up to the trail and to Dave's estate. "If you wanted to make a fast getaway this sand would slow you down, wouldn't it?" I asked as I slogged my way through deep, dry sand.

"That's for sure," Jack said scanning the area around him as he joined me. "Our walk was a lot easier on the wet, hard-packed sand near the water's edge."

"Fleeing up these steps wouldn't be easy either.

Attacking Dave from the cliff top would have avoided the need to do that." After we'd moved up some of the steps, I looked up to see how many more we had to climb. I glimpsed movement above us. I shifted over to one side to accommodate two-way traffic if someone was heading down toward us from the top of the stairs.

"Walking down the stairs would have been much easier if Dave's killer didn't have another escape route planned up there on the trail," Jack suggested.

About half way up the stairs, I stopped again, and settled on the spot where Dave's body had landed. I felt a moment of dread. Jack who stood a couple of steps below me had fixed his eyes on that spot, too. Then he peered up to the top of the cliffs and back down again. He must have been trying to pinpoint the place where Dave had gone over the edge.

I followed the path Jack's eyes had travelled. Suddenly, there was movement again, and this time I glimpsed a figure clad in dark clothing. Whoever it was, stepped back from the cliff's edge, gone from my view in an instant. Jack's voice startled me as he spoke now from the step just below the one I was on.

"I don't see how he could have landed as far away from the cliff face as he did unless he had some momentum when he fell." Jack stepped up next to me and made motions with both hands as he spoke.

"Like the momentum you'd get from a hefty shove, right?"

"Yep!" Jack was about to say more when his eyes turned upward. "Georgie, down, now!" As he issued that warning, he practically picked me up off my feet in an unexpected display of strength. We hustled down those stairs, side-by-side, with Jack's arm still around my waist. A spray of dirt and rocks poured down around us. I was enveloped in a cloud of dust as my back and legs were pummeled by ricocheting pebbles and grit.

Jack twisted a little to look up behind us, nudging me down to a step below him, providing cover as we continued moving toward the beach as fast as we could go. From above us, I heard what sounded like a cross between a growl and a grunt of rage. In the next instant, I glimpsed a big white plastic bucket hurtling through the air. I heard it bounce, and then caught sight of it again as it careened off the railing before rolling to a stop near the foot of the stairs.

When we reached the beach, I found out I could run in that dry sand after all. I was breathing heavily by the time we took shelter behind the closest outcropping of large boulders.

"What was that?" I asked, peeking up over the boulders to scan the cliff top and stairs. There was no sign of movement. A pile of stones and dirt lay on the steps near where we'd been standing when Jack had cried out for us to move. Some of the rocks on those steps weren't mere pebbles like the ones that had hit us as we fled.

"I'd say it was an invitation to take a hike somewhere else," Jack replied. Jack reached up and ran his hand through his hair, clearing out dirt that had settled in it. As he did that, I noticed a tiny little dribble of blood forming at the hairline on his forehead.

"Jack you're hurt! Are you okay?" I took a tissue

from a pocket of the cross-body shoulder bag I had on. Glad that I'd decided to bring it with me, I dug around a moment longer and found hand sanitizer, too.

"I'm fine," Jack said.

"I'll be the judge of that," I protested as I examined him. The process of cleaning him up was awkward. Jack already had his phone out and was calling his new pal Hank. The blood appeared to be coming from a tiny little scratch, so I left Jack alone to finish his phone call. It must have gone directly to Hank given how quickly I heard Jack utter his name in an excited tone.

"Hank's sending someone out to have a look around. I'm sure it's too late to catch the person who delivered that nasty invitation. Maybe the idiot made a mistake by pitching the bucket at us and it has some identifying information on it. It's a longshot, though."

"I heard you give Hank a description of the guy who did this. Is that why you turned around in the middle of the rockfall?"

"Yeah, I couldn't resist trying to get a look at the culprit."

"I ought to chew you out, Sir Jack of Crystal Cove! That must be when you got that new hole in your head. I appreciate your fleetness of foot and the fact you shielded me from the attack. But what good would all your chivalry have done me if you'd let the Black Knight strike you a mortal blow?" Jack smiled and wiped what must have been a smudge of dirt from my face.

"Black Knight means you must have seen him, too, huh?"

"Only for a split second," I replied. "I didn't see much. A person wearing dark clothes, not necessarily black."

"I didn't see much more than you did. A figure in dark clothes, wearing sunglasses, a hoodie, and gloves—like a boxer or like the Unabomber character in that police drawing. That's not a lot to go on to nab the guy. In fact, I didn't see a mustache, so I can't even be certain it was a man."

"It's good that you have quick reflexes. I shudder to think what could have happened if we hadn't been on the move already when those rocks hit the steps. Man or woman, it took keen eyesight and good control to get them to land as close to us as they did. That means it had to be someone who's big and strong, or in excellent physical condition, to dump a hefty bucket of rocks on us."

"I agree. As soon as Hank or his people get here, let's go find out if Adam Middlemarch is as big a guy as you remember. I'd also like to know where he was the past half an hour or so."

Jack had barely finished that sentence when we caught sight of a jeeplike vehicle heading toward us on the beach. A flashing light, signaled that the cavalry had arrived. It only took minutes more for Jack to show Hank and the young Lost Hills officer, Tony, around. I tagged along behind them, listening and observing, as they examined the scene. Tony took photos. I did, too, although I wasn't sure why. No one stopped me, so I snapped away. When Tony moved the bucket with a gloved hand, I leaned in to take a photo.

"What's that?" I asked. Jack and Hank stepped

closer to where Tony and I stood peering at that bucket. The plastic white bucket looked like many I'd seen being used for all sorts of tasks. This one now had a big split in its side. It bore no identifying letters or other marks which might help figure out where it had come from or what it had been used for before it had been weaponized. I pointed to a tiny slip of torn paper poking out from under the bucket.

"It's a shred of paper with musical notes on it," Hank responded, using a gloved hand to pick it up and place it into a clear plastic evidence bag.

"Good eyes, Georgie!"

"Here's another one. I'm going to see if I can find more down here, then I'll poke around up there in that pile of rocks and dirt," Tony added, walking toward those stairs and searching the sand as he went.

"May I take a closer look?" I asked as Hank turned the plastic bag over, examining its contents.

"Sure." Hank held it out for me to see. I could make out a series of musical notes. I hummed the first few bars of music to myself. I tapped out notes with my fingers pressed against my side as if I were playing a piano the way I'd done when taking lessons eons ago. In seconds I had it!

"I could be wrong, but I'd bet those are notes to a song Dave wrote for a movie called *Anytime, Anywhere*. The movie's theme song was *Anywhere You Go*, a name based on an old Confucian quote: *'No matter where you go, there you are,'*" I said.

"Uh, I'm pretty sure your maestro stole that line from another movie: In *The Adventures of Buckaroo Banzai Across the 8th Dimension*, Buckaroo Banzai uses it," Tony assured me as he reached the point where

Jack and I were standing when the rocks had begun to rain down from above us.

"You wouldn't be the first one to accuse Dave Rollins of stealing a line or two, but I doubt he stole it from Buckaroo Banzai in this or any other dimension. The story he shared with the public at his concerts had something to do with Confucius." I shrugged not sure what else there was to say. Jack knew me well enough to recognize irritation in my response. He decided to goad me. When I'm peeved, he finds my efforts to be polite amusing and likes to test my patience.

"I'm with Tony. I heard it from Buckaroo Banzai," Jack added with a smirk.

"You did?" I asked distractedly, as the fingers of my hand still hanging at my side, beat out the tune again.

Dang it! That song's going to bounce around in my head all day now, I thought.

"When was that movie made? Maybe Buckaroo stole it from Dave Rollins." This time the exasperation in my tone was obvious. I wasn't the only one growing crabbier.

"If a saying like that has been around since Confucius, who knows who stole what or when? Does it really matter?" Hank had been quiet, but he was cranky now. This probably wasn't how he'd planned to spend his day off. I regretted my premature happiness about our lazy Sunday being better than our sad, dreary Saturday.

Fortunately, Tony called out to us, freeing me from replaying more of Dave's song or stewing about a good day going bad. The interruption also ended the pointless debate about who first used that phrase. The three of us moved to the foot of the steps and looked up to where Tony stood on the stairs taking more photos of the pile of rocks.

"There are few more shreds," he said. "How do you want to handle this?"

"I'll help you collect them," Hank offered. "Jack and Georgie are going on up to the house. Not that there's been any trouble there, according to Georgie's latest call to her friend."

What he said was true. Once Jack had called for help, I'd called Pat again to make sure no growling, dirt-covered lunatic was throwing rocks at her or at Dave's house. I'd also sort of established that Adam Middlemarch wasn't likely to be our bucket-wielding assailant. When I asked Pat if she'd had any trouble or unexpected visitors, she'd said no. Without any prodding from me, she'd added that she *and Adam* were almost finished going through the wreckage on the second floor. I shared that bit of information with Jack, who just nodded in acknowledgement.

I was relieved Pat was okay. On the other hand, it sure would have made things easier if she'd told us Adam had taken off and was no longer at her side. At least we would have had a suspect in our hunt for someone angry enough to resort to throwing rocks at us to get us to go away.

"Once you've collected all those scraps, can you send us a composite photo of what you've found? We'll show it to Pat. Maybe she can tell us more about what's been shredded and where it came from."

"Sure, but that won't happen today," Hank grunted as he pulled another small evidence bag from a pouch he carried and bent down to pick up the scrap of paper Tony was pointing out. "You'll let me know if anything new turned up as they waded through the mess left behind in that house, right?"

"Yep!" Jack replied. "Is there room for us to squeeze by on those stairs without disturbing your work or do we need to get to the house some other way?" Hank took a quick look.

"If you're careful." Tony let out a puff of air as if he had something to say.

"What? It's dirt, for crying out loud! We'll take a sample in case the lab rats can use it to figure out where the heck it came from, but otherwise we're not going to get much from it. I'm planning on having you sweep it onto the ground to clear the steps once we've made sure there aren't any more paper shreds."

Jack moved quickly up those steps, perhaps wanting to get to the top before Hank changed his mind. I hustled as fast as I could, too. As I passed Hank, I heard him muttering to himself about dirt and rocks and litter. We only had a few more steps to go when a noise from above caused us all to freeze in place.

8 DAVE'S DEVOTED FAN

"Hank," a voice cried out. "We've picked up a guy in a hoodie and sweats. You want to send those folks up here…" He stopped mid-sentence when he stepped into view at the top of the stairs and spotted us on our way up. My heart thumped from the exertion but had also revved up at the prospect of coming face-to-face with our attacker.

"Where is he, Murray?" Hank hollered from below.

"At the maestro's house on the lower level deck. Mike Benson's holding him. That Personal Assistant came running out when she heard us shouting at the guy. We told her what was going on, and she said Detective Wheeler and the Shaw woman were on their way to the house."

"And so, we are," Jack said, hustling up the stairs. I scrambled up behind him hoping that our attacker and Dave Rollins' killer might be in the hands of the police. That hope dimmed the moment I caught sight of the wisp of a man Mike Benson had seated at a table on the maestro's veranda.

His clothes were soiled enough to believe he'd filled a five-gallon bucket with dirt and rocks. Still, he was so scrawny there was no way he could lift forty pounds, much less dump it on us. His weathered skin and the worn-out expression in his eyes had me convinced, at first, that he was my age, or close to it. As he spoke, and I took a closer look at Charlie Daniels, I guessed he was more likely in his thirties.

"It wasn't me! You've got the wrong guy."

"The wrong guy for what?" Jack asked.

"I don't know. Whatever you think I done that someone else done that wasn't me because I haven't done nothing I shouldn't a done." Charlie twitched as he spoke, growing more anxious, and more aggravated too if I was reading him right.

"How do you explain the oversized dirty gloves you have on and the signed picture of Dave Rollins?" That was Murray posing the questions—Officer Murray Oates as we'd learned once we'd made our way through the back gate and onto the maestro's sprawling patio.

"The wolfman gave 'em to me back there on the Bu cliff trail." I opened my mouth to speak. Bu's a term some locals use for Malibu, so that term didn't surprise me.

"Wolfman?" I burst out, speaking the word as if it were a question. "You're not serious, are you?" In the next instant, a stream of Marvelous Marley World characters sprang to mind, one after the other. Could someone in a character costume have been roaming around out there on the trail or had the jerk who'd attacked us put one on in his effort to escape? "You don't mean Wee Wily Wolf, do you?"

All eyes were upon me. Puzzled expressions in them, although Jack couldn't hide a twinkle of amusement in his. Charlie was incredulous, but at least he knew to whom I was referring.

"You think I don't know enough to tell you if it was Wee Wily Wolf and not a man?" He shook his head. "The guy who gave me the gloves and the picture had on running clothes with a shirt under his jacket that said wolfman. Or something like that. I might a seen him someplace before, but he wasn't Wee Wily Wolf. Now you've got me confused."

At that moment, I heard voices from inside Dave's house. Pat and Adam came to the back door. They both joined us on the veranda.

"Charlie, what are you doing out there?" Adam asked. Charlie stared at Adam Middlemarch, his eyes widened as though wary at first.

"You know this gentleman?" Jack asked.

"Oh, yes. He's a devoted fan of the maestro's," Adam replied smiling at Charlie. Dave's devoted fan relaxed. "He knows every song Dave Rollins ever wrote—by heart! Dave and I have both heard him sing some of them. Charlie has given me a hand a time or two when he was hanging around out front on the street singing, and we invited him in."

"That's where we found him—on the street in front of the house," Mike Benson offered. "He wasn't singing."

"I will if you want me to, but I don't feel like it. Dave told me he liked my singing. I'm sad he's dead." Charlie's furrowed brow and downturned mouth reflected the sentiment expressed by those words.

"We're sad, too," I said in a soft tone. I was not only sad about Dave's death, but the fact that his killer was still out on the loose. "Where did you meet up with the wolfman?"

"At the overlook about an hour ago," Charlie responded, pointing in the direction we'd come from when we climbed those stairs, although the overlook was a little past the point where the stairs met the trail. "Maybe it wasn't even an hour. I don't wear a watch." A little shiver rolled down my spine. The timing was about right. Surprising though. If I'd just unloaded a bucket of rocks on a couple of people, I'd have run for it.

"What did the wolfman look like?" I asked, hoping Charlie's response wouldn't have anything to do with "big and hairy with sharp teeth," or I figured our conversation would be over.

"Ordinary. About as tall as me, but bigger— especially in the belly. Too much beer," Charlie said patting his own flat, almost concave, abdomen.

His notion of what was a big belly might be a whole lot different than mine, I thought.

"Thanks," Jack said. "Anything else you can remember, like the color of his hair or eyes. Did he have a scar or a tattoo or any marks on him like that?"

"He had real dark sunglasses on and his hood was up. I could only see a little hair—it was white." A word Jack had used when we were still down on the beach ricocheted through my mind—Unabomber. Charlie's description fit.

"Blond, like Officer Benson here?" Murray asked. Charlie scowled at the officer, shook his head and rolled his eyes upward.

"I said white, not blond. White like Santa Claus, you know?" Another surge of disappointment hit me. I doubted the rock thrower was a senior citizen with a beer belly. My hope dimmed that Charlie had in fact seen the man who'd sent us that message in the form of a bucket of rocks, but I kept at it.

"Are you saying he was an older man?" I prodded.

"Older than me, but not as old as him." Charlie pointed to Jack when he said that. "It is strange he had white hair, huh? Okay, so maybe not ordinary."

"Do you remember what color clothes he had on?" Murray posed that question.

"Dark. More blue than black like the gloves he gave me because he said I looked cold. I thought he was being nice. Now I wish he'd left me alone. The top part had a zipper that was mostly unzipped. That's how I saw the wolfman shirt. It was red with this fancy writing on it."

"How about the picture? Where did that come from?" Murray asked.

"He gave it to me; only what he wanted to do was give it to me in pieces."

"What?" I asked thinking about the shreds on the beach.

"Yeah, crazy, huh? He was getting ready to throw it away. It fell onto the ground when he was cleaning out his backpack. I told him I wanted it and that's when he said, 'request it in pieces' or somethin' like that. I told him that was stupid. I wanted the whole thing or nothing. It's a signed picture! Dave already gave me one just like it, but somebody else will buy this one. I can use a few bucks." Charlie shrugged.

"How come you let it get dirty if you planned to sell it?" Murray asked.

"I didn't do that. It was already dirty. The backpack he had with him was full of trash. He must have been digging down on the beach with the shovel he had and got everything dirty like his gloves. The guy had one of those cool metal detectors in there, too."

"Small enough to fit in his backpack?" Jack asked, sounding skeptical. Charlie nodded.

"Yes."

We'd watched some guy on the beach in Crystal Cove beachcombing recently. The device the man had used folded up, maybe small enough that it could have fit into a backpack. It was certainly much smaller than the ones that had intrigued me when I was a child. I'm not sure what difference it made in determining whether the wolfman was our rock thrower. The shovel fit if that's what he'd used to load the bucket.

"Um, okay. Officer Benson's going to take your statement, for the record. Start at the beginning. Tell him when you ran into the wolfman, and exactly where you were, too." Then Jack turned and spoke to the officer.

"Mike, before you take that statement from him, why don't you have Charlie show you where the guy dumped the trash. Let's get the CSIs to come and collect the garbage and maybe it'll help us identify the wolfman." Now Mike was the one who wore a skeptical expression.

"Hey, it's not likely, but it's worth a shot. I don't

think that guy was a beachcomber looking for lost wedding rings, do you?" Jack asked.

"He wouldn't have filled the bucket on the beach and hauled it up all those stairs," I added. Mike looked at me for a moment and then nodded.

"On our way to the overlook, we'll see if we can find a place where he might have filled it. He can't have hauled it far from where he stood at the top of those stairs, either. He wasn't very smart if he was just standing around chatting with Charlie after what he did to you two." It's as if Mike had read my earlier thoughts. Charlie's eyes widened.

"Did he try to get you to request it in pieces, too?" Charlie asked looking at me and then at Jack. "That's not against the law, is it?"

I shook my head no, wondering once again why the guy would have asked Charlie such a thing. One lost soul trying to connect with another, perhaps, and babbling incoherently. Or Charlie had it wrong which seemed more likely.

"Don't worry about it, Charlie. Let's go. Who knows how long it will take for the county to get someone out here to go through the garbage." Charlie was not going to argue with that order from Mike. He was on his feet, still hanging onto that picture.

"You can take Charlie's statement while you're waiting," Jack suggested. "We're going to need that picture, though."

Charlie objected to that and held it close to his chest. Someone needed to end this so Mike and Charlie could get back to that garbage can before someone could empty it. I dug out my wallet, hoping

I had some cash.

"Charlie, I'm going to buy it from you, okay? How much do you want for it?"

"Five bucks," Charlie replied hastily, holding that photo out for me.

"All I have is a ten—how about you take that as payment for those gloves, too?"

"Deal!" Charlie grabbed the money, grinning. That smile made him appear much younger. I hoped he wouldn't do anything stupid with that ten dollars. He could use a decent meal.

Jack put on another pair of latex gloves he had in his jacket pocket and carefully placed the picture into an evidence bag. The gloves went into another one.

"Murray, will you take these to Hank, please, and let him log them in?"

"Sure."

"That was quick thinking, Georgie. I doubt we'll get a fingerprint from that picture even if the guy who gave it to Charlie handed it to him after removing his gloves, but who knows?"

"Those CSI guys are wizards. Maybe there's something on the inside of the gloves. What do we do with Charlie?" Mike Benson asked.

"Charlie are you willing to let the CSIs take a DNA sample?"

"To rule me out, right? Like on those TV shows?"

"Right!" I responded without thinking. Charlie wasn't as far gone as he'd seemed. "He's got that right, doesn't he, Jack?"

"Yes. Charlie, tell Officer Benson how we can

get in touch with you again, okay?"

"Like for a lineup so I can pick out the wolfman? That would be cool!"

"Maybe something like that," Jack replied. Then he spoke to Mike. "When he's taken you to that dump site and given the CSIs that sample, let him go. I don't see a reason to hold him."

"That's good to hear. Charlie's okay." Jack and I both turned around to see Adam standing near the glass sliding doors that lead into the kitchen. In the excitement, I'd forgotten all about him and the fact that we'd originally come here to check on his whereabouts at the time we'd been accosted on the stairs. That seemed less important if our nemesis was a white-haired, wolfman with a paunch. Adam was indeed big enough to have done the dirty deed, but no white hair and no paunch.

"Where's Pat?" Jack asked. "We'd like to speak to the two of you."

"Pat wants to talk to you, too. Come on in and have a seat. She'll be here as soon as the insurance adjuster has left. Help yourself to some bottled water from the fridge if you're thirsty. Watch where you walk or sit. The place is still a wreck although I tried to clean up the food that was starting to stink."

"Thanks, Adam." I said as he headed from the kitchen into the great room." I slipped into a chair in the morning room where Pat and I had sat the day before.

"I could use some water. You want some?" Jack asked.

"Yes," I replied realizing that the dust and exercise had left my throat dry. That might also have been related to anxious thoughts that had occurred to me once I sat down and had a moment to catch my breath. "A wolfman with white hair, a potbelly, and dressed like the Unabomber," I harrumphed.

"So much for a pleasant Sunday stroll," Jack commented as he handed me a bottle of water and joined me at the table. "That'll teach us to change our plans."

"What I want to know is how the wolfman knew where we were going to be today to issue that invitation to go away?"

"I was wondering the same thing. Did you tell Pat we were planning to join her at the house using those stairs?"

"Not directly. When she said she was going to be busy with the claims adjustor a while longer, I'm sure I told her not to worry about it since we'd park in the beach lot and walk over to the house from there."

"Do you have any idea who was with her at the time?"

"No, but let's ask Pat."

"Ask me what?" At the sound of Pat's voice, I nearly jumped out of my skin. "I'm sorry, Georgie. You two have had a rough day, haven't you? I wasn't trying to sneak up on you."

"We were preoccupied, trying to figure out how someone knew enough about where we'd be to load up a bucket of rocks and dump it on us as we climbed up those stairs."

"Hmm, that's odd, isn't it?" As she asked that question, she went to the fridge for a bottle of water and then dropped into the chair next to me.

"I know you weren't alone when I called. Was

anyone within earshot when I told you we were on our way?"

"Roger Winters came with an army. He and his crew were standing around. They could all have heard me tell Adam you were on your way to join us after your walk on the beach."

"Where's your assistant now?" Jack asked.

"He's helping load art and collectibles into a van. Apparently, in addition to Roger's team, Jennifer asked a packing and storage crew to show up, too. I wasn't sure why she hadn't told me in advance, so I called and discussed it with her. She argued those items shouldn't remain in the house while the cleaning and restoration work gets done, especially since we don't know how an intruder got into Dave's house. Some items will get distributed to other people once the will has been read, so preparing them to be moved or shipped needed to happen sooner or later. Anyway, Adam always gets roped into helping when there's heavy lifting to be done."

"Did they ask for his assistance earlier in the day?" Pat's brow furrowed as she pondered Jack's question.

"Yes. They put him to work, off and on, moving furniture so they could take photos of the damage or asked for his help to locate items to be packed from the list Jennifer had given them. Most of the time he was with Roger Winters and me, but not the entire time."

"How much do you know about Adam?"

"Dave hired him, not me. I took him on as a helper at Dave's request. Adam worked at Marvelous Marley World in park maintenance and asked Dave for help moving into the performance side of the company. I can't tell you how that came about. Maybe they met at one of the open auditions the company offers every so often. According to Dave, Adam has a nice singing voice, but needs more professional training in music and performance. He's enrolled in a community college and taking voice lessons but quit his job at Marvelous Marley World."

"Does that mean he wasn't able to make the switch into the Entertainment Division?" Carol could find out easily enough, but I wanted to hear what Pat had to say.

"Yes. Dave told me he tried to talk Adam into staying put. He left in good standing and told Dave he'd try again once he's made more progress with his singing lessons."

"How's he making a living if he quit his job?" Jack asked.

"He parlayed his handyman work for Dave into jobs elsewhere. Adam gave me a few Middlemarch Home Maintenance business cards he had printed up to give to anyone looking for a handyman. He's not a very talkative guy, but flexible, dependable, and stays on task. I've never felt the need to get to know him better, personally, so I can't tell you much more about him."

"Okay. That's helpful. Thanks," Jack said. "Adam said you had something you wanted to tell us. What is it?"

"I found this." Pat did a quick look around, and then unwrapped a tissue exposing a single gold loop earring. "It's not mine. I wear clip-ons. Marla's ears are pierced, but I've never seen her wear anything like it, either."

"Where did you find it?" Jack asked as, like a magician, he pulled another little plastic evidence bag from a jacket pocket. Pat dropped it into the bag, hanging onto the tissue in which she had wrapped it.

"On the floor near Dave's desk. It was under papers that could have come from a box of stuff on his desk if it had been searched."

"Are there items missing?"

"I don't know because I'm not sure what was in it in the first place. Offhand, nothing I could see appeared to be very important. Old sheet music, notes about compositions he was planning to work on, and a hodgepodge of pictures and clippings, as well as programs from performances he gave or attended. Dave had written 'sort and file' on the side of the box with a black marker. There were a couple of file folders that needed to be refiled. Maybe he was going to pass it along to me." Pat sipped her bottled water before speaking again. There was wariness in her voice when she spoke again, and she lowered her voice almost to a whisper.

"With all the activity in the house today, that earring could have come from almost anywhere."

"That would explain why the CSI's didn't pick it up when they were in here yesterday. I'm glad you spotted it."

"I wondered about that, Jack. Given how many hours they spent here, how did they miss it?"

"You're not saying someone planted it?" I asked.

"I guess not. I'm just totally paranoid. The team that went through here could have dropped or dragged it from one place to another when they moved stuff or pulled it from walls or shelves to be packed for storage."

"Can the lab get DNA from it?" I asked Jack, eying the gold band. It was a simple loop of gold like you could find in most any jewelry store.

"Who knows? Even if they can't, you never know when a personal item like this might come in handy given where it was found." Jack slipped the little bag into a pocket. Just then, Adam Middlemarch rejoined us.

"What a day, huh?" Pat asked. The quick shift to another topic caught me by surprise. Was Adam on the list of people she had in mind when she asked about someone planting that earring? Without waiting for a reply, she stood. "Unless you have something that can't wait, I really need to get out of here and take care of a few errands. I can't put my life on hold completely. Call me if you have questions, Jack. I'll see you tomorrow at lunch, Georgie." With that, she left. "I know I don't have to remind you to lock up everything, Adam."

"No, you don't," Adam replied as he took the seat Pat had occupied.

I would have liked a few more minutes with Pat to tell her Marla Broussard had family photos she wanted to contribute for Dave's memorial. I also wanted to ask Pat if, as Marla suggested, she had a way to reach Dave's brother Bill or his Aunt Meg. I'd take it up with her at lunch tomorrow instead. For some reason, I felt it might be better to have that conversation without Adam sitting at the table.

I listened attentively as Jack quizzed Adam about his whereabouts on Friday night and during the day today. He had what sounded like a plausible alibi, claiming he'd gone to a club in Santa Monica after the gala—if it checked out. On the surface he was affable enough, but I sensed an undercurrent of annoyance or reluctance to speak. He answered Jack's questions quickly and politely, keeping his responses short as if he were being deposed by a lawyer.

That's an interesting skill for a guy like Adam Middlemarch to have acquired, I thought. Jack agreed when I brought it up on our way home. A background check by the police was in Adam's future. Who knew what that might reveal about the big man inclined to say so little? Or what Carol might dig up about him, for that matter.

9 NOT A ROLLINS

"The first mention I can find of *our* Dave Rollins is in Chicago. He's no classical violinist, though. See? That's him playing the standup base in a jazz combo. A skinny kid in his twenties—a real cool cat!"

Monday morning, I peered over Carol's shoulder and looked at the picture on her desktop computer. My Executive Assistant proved once again that she's a whizz when it comes to mining the data we have about people who work at The Cat Factory. At least, anyone who was hired to work in the US or Canada. Some of the overseas operations in the far-flung Marvelous Marley World Enterprises were less penetrable by Carol's inquiries.

"Is that something you dug up from the archive?" I asked.

"Yep. I've Googled him, too, though, and searched in all the nooks and crannies that cater to Hollywood gossip or the theater news. If the maestro had a past, he kept his secret well-hidden. There's nothing I can find about a Dave or David Rollins getting into any trouble in Louisiana in the years before he shows up in Chicago."

"Hmm, that's too bad, isn't it?"

"Or maybe Marla Broussard made it up! That's a nasty thing to do."

"I don't believe Marla Broussard's above being nasty. If she's got dirty secrets about Dave Rollins, I bet they won't be kept secret much longer now that he won't be around to write checks for her."

"Ooh! Writing checks as in blackmail or alimony?" Carol has a wicked sense of humor that borders on the macabre at times.

"Blackmail never crossed my mind. She brought up the check writing in the context of their divorce. Alimony or hush money, it probably felt about the same to Dave either way. If her story's true about women causing him trouble in his youth, he never developed much sense. Marla's a living testament to his lack of discretion."

"Oh, there's plenty of gossip about his relentless pursuit of women and how often his love life fell flat, hit a sour note, created disharmony or dis-chord. I could go on and on with the music-inspired, love-gone-wrong puns. You can't pin them on me either. Tabloids, celebrity magazines, online journalists and bloggers can't resist them."

"Thanks for warning me," I said. Carol has a penchant for punning. Mostly cat related puns given how often we refer to ourselves as working for The Cat at The Cat Factory. Catmmando Tom's not the only cartoon character responsible for the success of Marvelous Marley World, but he's the iconic figure that most often comes to mind when someone mentions the place. The cat superhero, Catmmando Tom, is our counterpart to Disney's Mickey Mouse.

As if on cue, another of Max's beloved cartoon characters, Lucky La Roo, strolled past Carol's desk and on down the hall leading to the elevator. It was the start of a Lucky La Roo parade as several more associates in oversized kangaroo costumes followed. I didn't particularly care for the name Max had chosen for his jaunty kangaroo explorer. To me it sounded more like a stripper or a gambler, but what do I know? Kids of all ages love the smart-mouthed, "ramblin' roo" whose adventures place him in one bout of trouble after another.

"Character Casting must have held a training session already this morning with a new spiel or routine," Carol commented as the herd of "La Roos" sauntered past the reception area. One of them caught her staring and called out, "G'day Mates, watch this!" After coming to a halt, Lucky La Roo rocked back on the tail that went with the kangaroo costume. Then the occupant must have hit a button or done something because in the next second he straightened up and bounded to the elevator as if on springs.

"Wow!" Carol stood and gave the character two thumbs up. Not to be outdone, Lucky's companions followed suit. One even managed to add a fancy spin into the mix. By now half a dozen of us were watching the astonishing performance. When the elevator opened, the herd of La Roos waved and then stepped inside. We gave them a round of applause.

"Ah! I love this job!" Carol exclaimed. "You can

'*always expect the unexpected at Marvelous Marley World,*' can't you?" she added in a sing-song voice, using one of Max's favorite taglines for ads promoting his whacky world.

"That's for sure, with Max at the helm anyway," I agreed.

"It's inspiring."

"Here's an inspiration for you. Why not see if you can track down one of the other guys in Dave's band? Their names are listed in the caption below that picture. Maybe they'll know more about Dave's past than Marla knows or is willing to share with us. She couldn't even tell us how to reach his brother Bill or his Aunt Meg after suggesting we speak to them."

"If Dave Rollins' death has disrupted Marla Broussard's cash flow, why would she give the more lurid details to you?"

"I hear you. Not until she gets herself a deal for a tell-all anyway. We can't afford to wait for the ghostwriter to finish penning her story if we want to find out what really happened in Louisiana. Let's see if you can track down the other members of the Windy City Jazz Quartet."

"Will do. Let me know what I can do to help Pat with the memorial service for the maestro. I can arrange orders for food and beverage once you all decide what's on the menu. Figuring out when and where you want to hold the event's important, too."

"Anywhere but the pavilion where we just held his retirement gala. Marla was adamant about that and I agree with her. It'll have to be held somewhere that musicians can perform. Pat's probably the best person to make decisions about the music and we'll need some sort of retrospective."

"You have that wonderful piece put together for his retirement. I don't see why you couldn't rerun that in a private remembrance room. Once you pick a venue, I can arrange to have the video set up."

"That's a good idea. Marla has offered to send us family photos. We can put those on display, too, along with still photos from Dave's career working for the cat. Let's also include those pictures you've found from his days in the jazz band."

"Will do. You and Pat know more about the VIPs who need to be on the guest list and whether they should get special seating. Flowers, too, but not too much like a funeral. Nothing as fancy or structured as the gala, either, I hope. A more casual, drop-in event would make it possible for Associates to show their respects during their breaks or lunch hour."

"Great ideas, Carol. I'll bet Max will love opening this event up to as many members of the Marvelous Marley World family as possible. Especially if he gets to preside over a kick off ceremony at the start of the day. We can do finger foods and beverages that are easy to eat on the run. Petit fours and little mini-cupcakes decorated with music notes and symbols. Now that we're talking about food, I wonder if there is some truth to Marla's claims that Dave's roots were in Southern Louisiana. A French heritage, like the Broussard he married. I never asked him how a man from Chicago developed such a penchant for French food. Maybe his love of the cuisine came to him via the Mississippi Delta or the Louisiana Bayou. New Orleans makes sense, too, given his love of jazz."

"Well, Rollins doesn't sound French, bayou or otherwise. If that's his real name." When Carol said that, it's as if a bolt of lightning struck me.

"You're a genius. Of course, it's not his real name. That explains why you can't find anyone named Dave Rollins involved in a scandal in Louisiana before he shows up in Chicago."

"I bet the guys in his band not only know more about what kind of trouble he was in when he arrived in Chicago and whether he changed his name. Maybe they know what his name was before he changed it," Carol suggested.

"Go for it! I'll ask Jack about following up on the prospect that Dave changed his name, if no one has come up with the idea already. I'm curious about how he pulled off a stunt like that when he came of age back in the 60s."

"There's a picture with him behind the wheel of a car, so he must have been issued a Driver's License. I'll bet it was easier to get one then without all the scrutiny you get today. Even now, though, once you've got a Driver's License, it's easier to get other forms of identification like a credit card, Musicians Union Membership Card, or a work permit."

"I'm sure you're right. If you keep poking around trying to find Dave's old friends in Chicago, I'll try to find out if he's had any recent contact with his brother or his Aunt Meg. Marla's convinced Pat knows how to reach them."

"If Dave changed his name to Rollins, Bill probably has a different last name. How old must Aunt Meg be with a nephew in his seventies?"

"Good question. Meg's not likely to be Rollins,

either, is she? Even if she isn't alive, she may have children or other family members who can tell us what went on in Dave's past. The same goes for his brother Bill."

"Dave must have trusted them if he stayed in touch after he left Louisiana. Why wasn't he more concerned that they'd give away his secret somehow or lead him back into the trouble he'd left behind?"

"I wish I knew. That's a great reason to track them down. Jack and I are meeting with Dave's accountant and his estate lawyer today. Maybe they know something about his life before he turned up as a jazz musician in Chicago."

"Accountants and lawyers are tough-nosed and tight-lipped." I laughed at the image her colorful phrases conjured up.

"That could be why the lead investigator was more than happy to have Jack interview them about Dave's finances and the settlement of his estate. I'm going along to encourage Jennifer and his attorney to share what they know about Dave's beneficiaries, so we don't miss anyone important to Dave as we plan his memorial."

"Let's hope they don't go all lawyerly on you and refuse to share the information when you ask for it."

"Better to share it with me than have Max have to ask them for it. This is a murder investigation, and the boss wants answers! He's my ace in the hole if they want to do this the hard way."

"That'll work. No one wants to face the wrath of "Mad" Max Marley when he's riled up. In fact, he's probably already issued the command for them to cooperate or else!" As Carol said that, she stomped her feet and thrust her arms to her side, with her fists all balled up just as Max does when he's in tantrum mode. With her sparkling eyes and pixie face, it was difficult for her to achieve Max's troll-like demeanor.

"Who needs a bad cop when you've got Max in your back pocket?" I exclaimed.

"Exactly!"

"If anyone's looking for me this afternoon, I'm hoping to be back at my office by four. Unless there's a line of people waiting to see me, let's plan to spend a few more minutes on the memorial event for Dave then. I'll try to help move things along at lunch with Pat, so we can get the event scheduled at least. It's no easy task to find a large venue around here at the last minute."

"Boy, do I know it! Max can always pull rank and rearrange people and events any way he wants, but that could lead to a catfight or a hissy fit. Given the sad circumstances surrounding Dave's passing, that would be *appawling! Pawsitively* embarrassing, too, if the media catches wind of the fact that the *fur* is flying around here!" She clawed the air. I rolled my eyes as Carol opened her mouth to continue.

"Oh, stop! You've made yourself *purrfectly* clear. I'll do my best to sort this out before Max can have a *catniption* fit." I made clawing signs back at her. "I've got to go, or I'll be late." As I stood up to leave, an image of Adam Middlemarch looming over Pat came to mind.

"There is one more person to put on your list of people to check up on. He worked here for a while before Dave hired him to assist Pat." I passed along what little additional background I had about Adam

Middlemarch. "He's not a high priority, so don't go to any trouble if nothing pops up right away. I'm not sure what it was, but something in the way he handled himself around Jack made me wonder if he's had previous experience with lawyers or law enforcement."

"If he's been an associate with us, it'll be a piece of cake to find out about his work history. That shouldn't take long at all. Finding out if he's had legal training or legal trouble might take a little longer. Still, consider it done!"

I rushed off smiling. Carol's always so upbeat. She has a real "can-do" spirit even when she's doing the most mundane tasks. I can't fathom how she's so undaunted by the challenge of planning a project like our memorial event for the maestro. It's big, last minute, and not a happy circumstance. As she pointed out, it's fraught with the possibility Max will give in to his dark side and suddenly live up to his "Mad" Max nickname. I vowed to face the tasks ahead with the same gusto!

10 WHO GETS WHAT?

Jennifer Wainwright's office door was open. She sat at a small round conference table near a row of windows in her spacious, well-appointed office. Her posture was perfect—like that you'd expect to see in a dancer. She was thin and willowy like one, too. The tailored suit she wore accentuated the angular set of her jaw and the clean crisp lines hid any trace of a woman who might give herself over to the movements of ballet or jazz dance. Not that she lacked grace when I'd seen her walk across a room. There was just an air of control about her in even her slightest movements.

The sort of control and precision you hope your accountant uses to monitor your money, I thought as Jack and I followed a receptionist down a short hallway.

Jennifer wasn't alone. A well-dressed young man sat across from her. His demeanor was less controlled. Fidgety even. I could imagine him pacing back and forth like a caged lion if he were standing rather than sitting. Jack whispered in my ear as we approached the office.

"That baby-faced kid can't be the maestro's estate attorney, can he?"

"We're getting old enough that anyone who's thirty-something seems wet around the ears," I whispered.

"I'm glad you said thirty-*something* because I definitely don't trust anyone under thirty." I nudged him because the young woman leading us to Jennifer's office probably hadn't yet reached the thirty-year mark.

When we entered the office, Jennifer's companion was seated across from her. He appeared older as we drew close and fell under his analytical gaze. A pleasant smile returned the youthfulness to his face, as did a little awkwardness in the way he rose from the table to greet us. He didn't quite have the power meet and greet handshake down.

"Hello, he said as he reached out and shook my hand with enthusiasm. "I'm glad to meet you, Ms. Shaw. I've heard so much about you from Max Marley. I'm Terry Pfister."

"It's nice to meet you, too, Attorney Pfister. Hello, Jennifer," I added as I sat down next to her. Before she could respond, Terry spoke to Jack.

"You must be Detective Wheeler. You've made quite an impression on Max, too, although I understand he hasn't known you long. He sings your praises: 'Jack Wheeler's a law man of another kind. One who doesn't mind getting down into the mud if that's what justice requires!'" As he made that pronouncement, he sounded like Max and ended with a gesture that was an exact replica of one Max used often. I smiled wondering how much longer it would take before caginess won out over his spirited appreciation for the absurd. Jennifer did not smile, and her posture straightened more, if that were possible.

"I'm sure Max appreciates your obvious admiration for his glibness and ability to deliver a message." Trust Jack to put the best spin on the lawyer's amiable greeting. Jennifer relaxed ever so slightly. "It's a pleasure. And, please call me Jack." When he and Terry had exchanged a hardy handshake, they both sat down.

"May I bring you some coffee or another beverage?" the receptionist asked.

"Coffee would be wonderful," Jack replied. I realized I could use some too. I'd skipped it at my lunch with Pat, ordering iced tea instead.

"I could use a cup, too."

"Just bring us a pot, Grace, please?"

"Sure, Skip. I'll be right back."

"Skip is what everyone around here calls me."

"Is it a childhood nickname?" I asked out of sheer curiosity.

"No. Before I had my law degree, I worked as a skip tracer. Somewhere along the way the name got mixed up with my own. I like Skip better than Terry, so I quit correcting people. Sometimes judges don't take kindly to the fact I have to clarify who I am. They don't always appreciate my bounty hunter past. It does make me a memorable law man, though." He pointed his finger skyward for emphasis, once again imitating Max.

"That background you have chasing down

fugitives must come in handy from time to time," Jack added. I wondered if the wheels were turning in Jack's head. Had Skip applied those skills to investigate Dave Rollins' past?

"I suppose I'd have an edge evaluating the risk that a client might run for it if I were handling criminal cases. Don't tell Max I said this, but I'm glad I don't have to get down in the mud in pursuit of justice. That got old quick. Occasionally, I get pulled into a case where there's some question about fraud related to the settlement of an estate. Believe it or not, this is the first time I've been asked to answer questions about a client who was murdered."

In that moment, the supposedly seasoned, mud-weary skip tracer looked younger than ever. His eyes widened making them appear rounder, exaggerating the roundness of his face. His gaze shifted abruptly as Grace entered the room with coffee. The aroma swirled around us as she poured a cup for each of us. Jennifer, who had been completely silent since Grace had left to fetch the coffee, took charge.

"Thanks, Grace. We'll help ourselves to cream and sugar if we need it. Would you shut the door on your way out, please?"

"Sure, please let me know if you need anything else."

As soon as the door closed behind her, Jennifer opened a portfolio and pulled out a sheet of paper for each of us.

"If I understood you correctly when you arranged this meeting, Georgie, your interest in meeting with us is twofold. First, you want to know who was involved with Dave Rollins in his later years who might have something to say about how Marvelous Marley World plans to honor his passing. Second, you want to know who stands to gain by Dave Rollins' death." I hadn't put it in such blunt terms, but she had it right.

"That's the gist of it," I agreed.

"It probably won't come as any great surprise that, for the most part, it's the same small group of people who qualify on both counts. I checked with Skip to make sure that was the case before I prepared the list of names and contact information for you."

Jack and I scanned the list she handed us. It included his children and his ex-wife and more than a dozen other people. Several of those names were new to me and I was eager to learn more about them. Several of the names on the list, like that of his agent Bernie, also noted each as the "recipient of a token bequest." I flipped the paper over, but there was no more specific information anywhere about what that meant or who got what.

"What's a 'token bequest'?" I asked. "I don't think I've ever heard that term used before."

"It's not a technical term," Skip replied. "By that, we mean that Dave has left a specific personal item and/or a small transfer of cash or other assets to an individual. For the most part, we're talking about personal items that are hard to price—like the framed copy of the first contract he ever signed with his agent and a few other personal items. That's true for a violin he's leaving to the first violinist in the Marvelous Marley World orchestra."

"That's quite a generous gift!" I exclaimed.

"It's no Stradivarius, but it's still valuable.

Collectibles aren't worth anything until someone makes an offer."

"I'm certain Richard Hart won't want to sell it. It's a lovely, hand-crafted instrument. Glorious to see but even more remarkable when played by a skilled musician. Dave mentioned once that it was one of his most valuable possessions because of its beauty not its price. It was right up there with those delightful Indian miniatures and the vintage sheet music he collected. I wonder who's going to inherit those items?" Jennifer scrutinized me closely as I made those remarks. Just as I was starting to feel uncomfortable, Skip spoke.

"I can provide you with more details about each gift if you think it's important."

"Would you do that, please?" Jack asked. "We're still early in this investigation and it's not clear what might turn out to be meaningful, but squabbling about who gets what often does, I'm afraid."

"Sure," Skip replied making a note to himself on the proverbial yellow legal pad.

"Pat mentioned that much of Dave's personal memorabilia had been moved to the Marvelous Marley World archives. I didn't pay close attention during the quick walkthrough Jack and I did at the house during our visit, Saturday morning. His collectibles still seemed to be in the locked display cabinet in his office. None of his artwork appeared to have been damaged or destroyed either."

"That's fortunate for everyone who stands to benefit from Dave Rollins' largesse," Jennifer offered. "I suppose we'll need a copy of the report from the insurance adjuster before we can make a final determination of how true that is."

"I take it they have a complete inventory of what Dave Rollins kept at his home and the condition of each item at the time they insured it," Jack commented as he jotted down a note on a pad in front of him: "insurance inventory—before and after break-in."

"That's true. Perhaps it's too early to breathe a sigh of relief on behalf of the maestro's beneficiaries," Skip added with a shrug. "We don't want anyone to be disappointed."

"Lawyers! They worry too much. Pat would have told us if she'd discovered something of value that had been stolen or damaged."

"When she spoke to you yesterday about your decision to have it all crated and moved into storage, you mean?" I asked, curious that she didn't bring that up. Jennifer's eyes narrowed as if sizing me up or the intent behind my question.

"Yes, that's a measure intended to protect Dave's assets from another incident. Pat had already been through the house with the police the day before. Has she contacted you since then, Detective?"

"No. What she reported was that not much of value *appeared* to be lost or damaged from her examination of the wreckage—even after taking another look at it yesterday. We'll wait to see what the audit reveals since it'll be more thorough, and then we'll get a final tally."

"We can send you a copy of the audit once we get it." Skip spoke, and Jennifer nodded.

"Don't go to any trouble. We'll have the insurance company send us a copy. It sounds like you won't rest easy about being able to fulfill Dave's intentions until you get it." Jack examined the list of beneficiaries. I did too. Perhaps, like me, he wondered what kind of flack Skip and others at his firm faced if they couldn't honor Dave Rollins' bequests because of vandalism or theft. Or who would make such a fuss? One name jumped out at me.

"How nice that Dave included Marla among his beneficiaries. Did she know she was on the list?" Killing him was a way to speed up getting her hands on whatever Dave had left her. She sounded sincere when she'd told us it would have been stupid to kill the golden goose writing those monthly checks. Was she more upset than she let on about having to ask for what was rightfully hers each month? Skip and his colleagues had better hope none of what was coming to her was missing or there would be a price to pay.

"Yes. When they divorced, Dave made provisions for Marla to have a share of the proceeds from the sale of the house in the event of his death. That wasn't a secret. His wealth is substantial, and his children stand to inherit the bulk of his estate. Ensuring that their mother benefited from the sale of what was once their family home was a little sentimental but didn't have much impact on the disposition of his assets. Those assets also include royalties from the music he wrote as well as any money that might come from licensing agreements or other uses to be made of his name and musical legacy."

"Offhand, do you have an idea of what he's worth?" Jack asked.

"Jennifer can probably give you an estimate of

his current net worth down to the penny, but I'd say upward of eighty million dollars." Jennifer nodded in agreement. Jack let out a little whistle.

"It's good to work for The Cat!"

"Dave wrote hundreds of songs and more than a few of them made tons of money for Marvelous Marley World. Dave retained the copyrights and Max saw to it that Dave got his cut of any royalties that came from recordings. If you factor in his future earnings, it could be much more than that. For a legendary figure like Dave Rollins, he's likely to make much more money dead than alive. That depends on how well his life's work is managed, which is one reason he set up Music Man Enterprises before he died."

"Will the family run the business?" I asked.

"Marla and each of Dave's children already own shares in the business. His holdings will be divided among them. The business is run, day-to-day, by professionals with knowledge and experience in the entertainment industry. The managers of MME report to a board. Jennifer and I sit on the board, along with Dave's son and daughter. Marla, too, as do several representatives from the creative arts—music, film, and theater. Dave Rollins also has a Charitable Foundation and a member sits on MME's board. Marvelous Marley World always has two seats since The Cat Factory's reputation is also at stake depending on how Dave's music is used."

"Do the board members get compensated for their duties?"

"Some do. I don't take money because I get paid to manage Dave's personal estate—the family's estate now. Jennifer doesn't either since she has a similar role to play on the accounting side. Marla and the kids don't take money. Nor does anyone from Marvelous Marley World. That still means about half the members are paid a six-figure salary for their service."

"Wow!" Jack exclaimed at the numbers being tossed around.

"Pat's mentioned here," I said going back to the list Jennifer had given me.

"Yes. Dave made provisions in his will for her. I forgot to include her as a board member, didn't I? As his longtime Personal Assistant, she's always been concerned about protecting his legacy. She probably knew him as well as anyone alive, and she's fiercely loyal. Marla didn't always appreciate Pat's presence, but Dave had the last word on the matter, so they've made it work." Skip shrugged.

"Does she get paid?"

"She tried to refuse, but Dave insisted that she accept compensation. I'm sure that's as much as she earns from her annual salary as his PA. Dave also set up a retirement fund for her years ago, but the extra compensation from her seat on the board was intended to make it easier for her to prepare for that eventuality. She's younger than Dave, but older than his ex-wife. He valued Pat's years of service and wanted to provide for her in the event of his death."

"That board seat gives her a pretty good retirement income," Jack offered.

"Yes, and then there's the cottage. She'll have a place to live in retirement, too," Skip added.

"The cottage?" I asked. "Do you mean the one Dave Rollins was renting when Pat first met him?"

"You know about that, huh?" Jennifer asked, smirking. The smirk turned into a smile as she continued to speak. "Dave Rollins was a hopeless romantic. As his accountant, I objected to the offer he made on that beach house. Cottage is a nice word for what was more like a rundown shack. He insisted on purchasing it when he heard it was up for sale, concerned that someone might buy it for the location and tear it down."

"Given the price of property near the beach, I'm sure he was right," I added.

"He not only bought it but fixed it up. It's got the same cozy feel it always had but it's structurally sound—a little bigger than it was—and has been totally updated."

"Jennifer's like a proud mom," Skip interjected. "She had a hand in the redesign and renovations." Jennifer's whole demeanor shifted, as if she'd let her hair down or a box that had enclosed her suddenly fell away.

"I probably should have been a designer rather than an accountant. It was a pleasant way to reconnect to my artsy side."

"The bottom line is that Dave left that cottage to Pat. Before you ask, no she doesn't know. It's going to come as a surprise to her when we reveal the details of his estate."

"That's quite a nice surprise!" I exclaimed.

"Please, let's keep it that way, okay? It's one way we can honor Dave's intentions," Jennifer implored. I nodded.

"Sure," Jack replied. "Are there going to be any other surprises at the reading of the will?" Jennifer and Skip looked at each other.

11 FOLLOW THE MONEY

"When his granddaughter shows up, that ought to create a stir," Jennifer responded. I suppressed a gasp but couldn't keep the astonishment from my voice.

"Granddaughter—he has one?" I asked. I'd once overheard Dave bemoaning the fact that Katie was opposed to the idea of ever having children, and Carter wasn't likely to make him a granddad either since he'd filed for divorce.

"Yes. He didn't realize it until recently when Maggie Knight found him. Her name is on the list." Skip hesitated. Jennifer let out a big sigh and took over where Skip had stopped.

"This is a story that Dave was trying to keep under wraps, even though most of the people involved are no longer alive. I don't have all the details, but when Dave was a very young man he became involved with a woman. She was a little older than he was at nineteen, and she was already married.

Nowadays, in and of itself, adultery wouldn't be such a shocker, but in the 1960s—especially when it was the woman who was unfaithful—it was devastating. Dave's family was furious that he'd put the family name and reputation on the line. They ordered him to leave the house and never return. That's about as much as Dave told me. When Skip snooped around, he found out more."

"His name wasn't Dave Rollins, but Daniel Devereaux. At least part of the family's outrage was about the fact that the woman's husband, Robert Landry, came from a family that had made their money importing liquor during Prohibition. He was still involved in illegal activities like hijacking goods being brought in through the gulf. He ran night clubs that hosted backroom gambling operations along with other illicit sidelines. Dave used to sneak around and visit those clubs as a teenager. That's where he discovered jazz and took up the bass. A few years later when he started playing in one of those clubs, he fell for the boss's wife. Some of the trouble was detailed in local papers, along with the fact that it got nasty, and Daniel Devereaux ended up in the hospital after a beating. My guess is, he was told to leave town and figured that was no guarantee they'd leave him alone unless Daniel Devereaux ceased to exist." Skip may have intended to end his story there, but Jack had questions for him. I did too.

"Probably not a bad idea. Robert Landry sounds like a dangerous man. If Maggie Knight is Dave's granddaughter, does that mean he also has a daughter somewhere?" Jack asked.

"I don't believe Dave ever knew she existed until recently. She was born after he left Louisiana."

"*Eight months* after he left," Jennifer added. "It's possible that Landry's wife didn't know she was expecting a child when Daniel took off, left his old identity behind, and transformed himself into Dave Rollins," Jennifer added.

"Or she kept it to herself to protect him from her husband given the situation had already become bad enough for Dave to end up in the hospital. Who knows what a man like Robert Landry would have done if he'd discovered his cheating wife had become pregnant," Skip offered.

Or might still do if he's alive and aware that Maggie Knight found out Dave Rollins was Daniel Devereaux, I thought. "What a sad story. Where is his daughter's name on this list?"

"She's not. That's another sad tale. Dave's daughter, Deidre Landry, was bad news. On trial for murdering her husband, Harry Knight, before she was thirty, a hung jury kept her from going to prison. There were rumors that Robert Landry paid off jurors to get that outcome. Anyway, getting away with murder didn't mean she turned her life around. She was dead from a drug overdose not long after the trial ended." Skip shook his head. "Some people just can't learn, can they?"

I couldn't help thinking that went for Dave, too. Some men might have learned to be more judicious in matters of the heart after being disinherited and driven from home by scandal and a beating. Not Dave Rollins.

"Who took care of their daughter, Maggie?" I asked.

"Her grandmother, for whom she was named.

Margaret Landry passed away recently which may explain why Maggie looked up her granddad after all these years. Her *biological* grandfather, I guess I should say, since she grew up believing Robert Landry was her grandfather. Dave and Maggie didn't say how she found out about Dave, but Margaret Landry wouldn't have been the first person to reveal a family secret on her deathbed." Skip shrugged.

"What about Robert Landry?" Jack asked. His mind must have ventured down the same path as mine. If Dave's granddaughter had tracked him down, why not someone with an old grudge to avenge?

"He was killed years ago. In true mob boss fashion, Robert Landry was gunned down in a warehouse near the docks in Gulfport. Maggie was still just a toddler when that happened so I'm not sure how much she remembers about him or his death. Given the circumstances surrounding the way in which he died, it was big news at the time," he added.

"Did Dave ever say any of that old news had intruded into his life before his granddaughter showed up?" Jack asked.

"No, but I was his accountant and friend for more than twenty years. He revealed little to me about his past life until Maggie's arrival on the scene recently. I'm not sure if that's because he was trying to spare Marla and the kids embarrassment about his past, or if he was still concerned about revenge."

"It's hard to believe anyone else cared enough to kill him decades later if Robert Landry's dead." I wondered aloud.

"My sentiments exactly," Skip interjected. "When Dave grabbed the spotlight as the maestro, he was a much older man than he'd been when he left town as Daniel Devereaux. Maybe no one noticed or made the connection. Robert Landry's buddies in the Dixie Mafia, or whatever moblike group they were affiliated with, were all on the same flameout career path to an early death. Besides, Dave wasn't the kind of guy who would stand by and allow himself to be threatened by someone wanting to settle an old score or a new one. A rich, high profile figure like Dave Rollins was often targeted by one louse or another, and he was quick to act when that happened."

"Targeted how?" Jack asked, now on alert.

"By people charging him with copyright infringement or otherwise stealing intellectual property. That included some who claimed he stole music or lyrics from them. Breach of contract claims, too, from younger people in the entertainment industry who said he promised to make them a star or otherwise advance their careers and failed to do so. Mostly jilted girlfriends, but others he'd mentored or worked with—male and female. None of his disgruntled or disappointed complainants ever delivered heavy-handed threats like having his knees broken or anything so unsightly as the beating he took in his youth. No threats that I know of to extort money or blackmail him, probably because it wouldn't have worked given how much scandal Dave created for himself over the years. I'm referring to what I'd call ridiculous claims and 'frivolous lawsuits.' Dave often settled out of court to end the dispute, a commonplace practice among the rich and famous."

"How about threats from overzealous fans or stalkers?"

"Yeah, those too. By mail or email, as far as I know. He never complained to us about anyone confronting him in a hostile way in a public setting or sneaking into his house or onto the grounds of his estate. An incident like that would have been primetime gold for the entertainment news if it had happened. Once he married Marla and they knew they were going to have a baby, Dave had the grounds of his estate enclosed and gated. Pat tried to get him to add video surveillance, but I don't believe he ever followed through." Skip stopped speaking and searched Jack's face as if waiting for my husband to confirm or disconfirm the existence of video footage. "If you had video of someone entering his house that night you'd have a suspect in custody by now, wouldn't you?"

"It's never quite that easy," Jack responded in a noncommittal way that left the matter open. Having been on the scene, I knew better. One of the responding officers told Jack and Sgt. Bardot there were no cameras.

"All you have to do is follow the money and you'll see how much Dave spent over the years defending his rights to the music he wrote or fending off claims that he stole a melody or lyrics from someone. I often thought the deals he cut were unnecessary and partly to assuage his guilt about not being a nice guy in certain areas of his life. He could be woefully insensitive toward the women in his life when his infatuation with them ended. The media badgered him constantly about his womanizing." Jennifer scowled as though there was a bad taste in her mouth. "Not always undeserved, I should add."

Her expression and the way she spoke made me

wonder how close a friend Jennifer had been to Dave. Maybe it was the depth of conviction in her voice when she uttered those words about Dave's insensitivity toward women. Had she learned that through personal experience rather than simply observing him as his accountant?

"I doubt the claims that he stole other musicians' work would have held up even if they'd gone to court. The settlement agreements brought issues to a close more quickly. They included nondisclosure clauses, too, so whoever was making accusations had to shut up about it. There won't be much in the public record about them. Dave didn't take legal action against all the kooky claims. The media might have been unable to resist the idea that to some poor self-proclaimed Mozart, Dave was Salieri. The guy harassed him from time to time," Skip added.

"Are you talking about the sort of rivalry portrayed in the movie, *Amadeus?*" I asked.

"Yes. Pat and Dave seemed more amused than disturbed about the situation. Apparently, the letters looked as if they were written in ink with an old-fashioned quill pen. I never saw them, but from Pat's description it sounded like calligraphy rather than typical handwriting with lots of flourishes. The rambling notes were always signed with an elaborate letter M."

"Does that mean there were no threats in them?"

"None that I ever heard about. If anything, the writer was the one who felt threatened. There were warnings that the would-be Mozart was wise to Salieri's poisonous intentions or some nonsense like that. If this matters to you, you'll have to ask Pat—

keeper of the Mozart letters." Skip shrugged.

"I'm surprised she hasn't mentioned it," I muttered wondering once again about Pat's reluctance to share details about Dave's life.

"Pat's not always as forthcoming as she appears to be. At least not when it comes to her role as Dave's Personal Assistant," Jennifer replied.

"What do you mean by that?" Jack asked.

"Let's just say that Pat can go overboard in her efforts to protect the maestro." Skip jumped in almost cutting Jennifer off.

"Jennifer and I disagree about this, but she believes Pat sometimes discouraged Dave from bringing matters to us or taking legal action when he should have done it. I doubt Dave ever let a woman tell him what to do. Like I said, Pat and Dave found their Mozart wannabe more laughable than threatening," Skip added.

"Are you saying no one was ever angry enough to refuse to settle or threatened to take matters into their own hands because of a professional rivalry, real or imagined?" Jack asked.

"Not that I'm aware of," Skip replied.

"Maggie Knight's arrival is proof that Dave hasn't been open about everything that's gone on in his life, isn't it?" Jennifer asked, tapping her pen on the yellow pad in front of her. Her agitation had me wondering if she was being less than candid with us.

"Jennifer's too polite to tell you how to do your business, Detective, but you could ask the same question about his relationships with women. He sometimes settled those disputes with money, too. Does that mean there aren't women out there who are happy to see him dead? I'm sure there must be. Who? I can't tell you that."

"The entertainment media might be more help to you on that front. They've kept track of every relationship that went sour in a public way."

"Thanks, Jennifer," Jack said. "We have someone who's been looking into the media stories about Dave." He meant Carol, of course, since I'd already mentioned the results of her research into Dave's social media presence involving his troubles with women.

"Have there been any new or recent allegations against him or any changes in the money the maestro paid out in relation to his old settlements—to disgruntled women, mentees, songwriters—anyone?"

"Nope! Nothing he discussed with me," Jennifer responded quickly. "If it was a small matter, he could have taken care of it from the household fund Pat manages for him. I'm not privy to his use of those funds, nor would I have become involved unless he needed a substantial amount of money, like he needed to purchase and renovate an old beach cottage last year. If the terms of an old agreement changed, the lawyers would have become involved too, right, Skip?"

Hmm, a household fund. That's interesting, I thought. Over lunch, Pat and I had discussed several tasks on her to do list that involved keeping Dave's house up and running until his estate could be settled. It hadn't occurred to me to ask how she could do that without access to funds. She'd made such a point about the fact that Jennifer handled the money, I assumed the accountant paid the bills.

"That's true about any formal agreements Dave had made. I can check just to be sure I haven't missed an update of an old settlement. Jennifer's making another important point, though. We tried to help Dave understand it was best to take all the complaints he received through our formal process rather than deal with them on his own. I'm afraid his artistic, impresario temperament worked against him. That not only got him into jams, but I suspect sometimes kept him from cleaning up matters in a transparent way. Good luck figuring all this out!"

"When did you last speak to Maggie Knight? Does she know Dave is dead and does she know his death is being investigated as a murder?" I asked.

"Only if she's picked up something via the media. We haven't spoken to her since she first came in here with Dave a few months ago," Jennifer replied. "I've provided two addresses for her, as you can see. One in Louisiana, but another in Ventura Beach. Skip and I didn't want to cross wires with the police investigation or the effort you and Pat are making, Georgie, to reach out to friends and family. In case you're wondering if she might have shoved him off a cliff to speed up her inheritance, she didn't need to do that since Dave had already set up a trust fund for her. That's how she can afford her beachside condo. She stands to inherit more, but she's set as it is."

I caught a sideways glance from Jack and could almost read his thoughts. "Set" is in the eye of the beholder, isn't it? He had a point. For some people, waiting to inherit more might not cut it. Was it purely a coincidence that Maggie Knight showed up, and not long after Dave changed his will to make her a beneficiary, someone kills him?

12 DAVE WAS DAVE

When I returned to my office, Carol was at her desk speaking to someone on the phone. I waved as I walked by where she sat in an office adjacent to mine. As luck would have it, one of Dave Rollins' sweeter tunes was playing in the background. Nostalgia washed over me as I settled in at my desk as the last bars of that song ended. Anger, too.

After we'd left our meeting with Jennifer and Skip, Jack shared a bit of shocking news as we returned to our cars. He'd received a copy of the statement issued by the coroner. The preliminary examination indicated Dave died between midnight and two a.m. Saturday morning. Someone had hit him on the back of the head. A forceful blow that might have killed him even if it hadn't propelled him off the cliff and onto the rocks below.

"How horrible!" In my mind, I'd run through the names on that list Jennifer and Skip had prepared for us. I didn't know everyone on it, but it was impossible to imagine any of the people I did know doing such a thing. I couldn't picture Jennifer bashing Dave over the head in a fit of rage even if their relationship hadn't always been a strictly professional one. I even had a hard time figuring Marla had done it now that we'd learned about her role as a board member at Music Man Enterprises and the provisions Dave had made for her in his will. They must have been closer than I realized, despite Marla's nastiness about having to pick up her check from him each month.

"The coroner believes that fall finished him off given the way he landed."

"You can skip the gory details, Detective." As I'd said that, I took his arm wondering how a man as wonderful as Jack could deal with such horrors on a regular basis. Violence of one kind or another, however, is a routine matter for the team he heads. Not murders, per se, since they don't happen that often in the OC where he works. Trust me, and my affiliation with Marvelous Marley World, to drag him into another one from another county altogether!

"I'm happy to let the forensics specialists deal with those details, too. What matters to me is that they've established he didn't just fall or jump."

"What about a murder weapon? Does the coroner have any idea what was used to strike that blow?"

"My guess is it was a piece of wood lying around up there. They found wood fragments in the wound."

"Oh, yuck. Sorry I asked." Jack had reached out and put an arm around me.

"Good luck finding it. The beach below is littered with driftwood that's washed ashore as well as branches deposited on the beach when rain washes them down onto the sand from the hillside. A quick toss off the cliff and it's well-hidden even if it's lying right out in the open!" Jack had demonstrated what he meant by gesturing as if he were flinging an object.

"The choice of weapon makes it seem more like a make-do kind of murder by an amateur, don't you think?"

"Not the work of a hitman paid for by the Dixie Mob, you mean?"

"Yes, I guess that's what I mean."

"I agree. A professional would have come better prepared and would have worked harder to make it look like an accident. Point a gun at Dave, get him to back up close enough to the cliff, and he falls or goes over the edge with a helpful shove. There's no need to bash him over the head." Jack had acted it out for me.

"Yeah, I get it. Maybe you were right that Dave's dream date turned into a nightmare. If he misjudged the woman with him, made his move, and she wasn't interested in romance, maybe she picked up a big stick to fend him off."

"A slap in the face for getting fresh probably would have brought the maestro to his senses given Pat's characterization of him as a cad rather than a predator."

"It was late and dark. She could have been scared. I guess if she started whacking him in a confrontation like that, he'd have injuries on his face or the front of his body, not the back of his head." It had been my turn to act out what I was saying, flailing my arms as though warding Jack off with a stick!

"You do have a point, wild woman!" Stepping closer, he'd wrapped his arms around me. "It's also possible someone was waiting for him or followed him on his moonlit walk and assaulted him. I wish we knew what happened to his romantic partner."

"You're not suggesting she was a murder victim, too, are you?" Jack let me go and shoved his hands into his pockets. That was a gesture I'd come to recognize as one he makes when he's feeling frustrated. Almost as if his hands were tied rather than shoved purposely into his jacket pockets.

"Let's hope not. It's more likely his date took off."

"Before Dave was attacked or after?"

"That's the first question we need to ask her if we can track her down, presuming she's still alive."

"It's odd she hasn't come forward now that the media frenzy has begun. She could be hiding out if she witnessed such a brutal assault."

"Hiding out won't necessarily keep her safe. Even if she got away unseen by the killer, the media is bound to figure out Dave had company at his home that night. I hope we find her before the reporters do and reveal her identity."

"Have you questioned the valets that were on duty that night? As I recall, there were people helping to manage the crowd as we all streamed out of there. Didn't any of them have anything to say about who was with Dave when he left?"

"We're working on it—give us a little time, will you?"

"Well, if you ask me, there are lots of people who should be coming forward who aren't doing it. The same people you're worried about who are likely to squawk to reporters ought to be offering to help the police."

"Let's hope people are just in shock. The media hasn't said a word yet about the fact that he wasn't alone Friday night. Maybe no one considered it important since wherever Dave went there was a woman or women with him. There had to be plenty of media coverage of the maestro's 'getaway' that night."

"That's a great idea, Jack! Marvelous Marley World had a videographer and photojournalist there, too, I'm sure. I'll get Carol to find out more for us."

"Maybe the paparazzi or local television news reporters caught something helpful on film and they're stalking Dave's woman friend as we speak." Jack's mention of stalking had suddenly given me the willies, and I began to turn around to look behind me.

"Stay put, Georgie," Jack said. "We're not in any danger, but we are being watched."

"Who? Where?"

"Jennifer's been keeping an eye on us. She's also been on the phone since she stepped over to her office window to observe our fascinating journey to the parking lot."

"Why?"

"I don't have an answer for you. I'll ask, but let's see what else I can dig up about her first. It'll help to have more context or a bit of leverage to use when I ask why she was so interested in keeping an eye on us after we'd left her office."

"Since she's going to so much trouble, let's make it worth it for her to spy on us. What do ya' say,

Copper? You want to curl her hair for her?" When I'd reached out to tug on Jack's tie and pull him closer, he was way ahead of me. Jack had crushed me to him and kissed me in a way that would have been a fitting end to any film noir romance scene. Even now, as I sat in my office, I reached up expecting to find a few new ringlets in my hair.

My ruminations ended abruptly when I realized I needed to speak to Carol right away. In addition to asking her to locate the corporate video and photo coverage of Dave's retirement gala, I had another task in mind. Carol's skilled at prowling for Cat Factory "back alley" chatter, as she likes to call it. Her "go to" place for all the latest "mews and views," including those not fit to print.

Jennifer's not a Cat Factory employee, but she's well-known to company associates given her ties to the corporate bigwigs. I don't use her firm's services because my father was an accountant and I'd long ago chosen an accountant he'd recommended. Like the maestro, many others in middle and upper management at Marvelous Marley World do. I hoped Carol could follow up and find something enlightening about my hunch that Jennifer and Dave had a personal as well as a professional relationship at some point.

Before I could act on my intention to speak to Carol, she dashed into my office. The petite, thirty-something woman stood in my doorway, almost vibrating with excitement.

"Georgie, you're going to want to hear this. I've got Teddy Austin on the phone and he's a talker!" Carol motioned for me to follow, and then took off.

"She can really move in those Princess Christiana high-tops!" I muttered as I followed her at what felt like a lumbering pace compared to the way she'd zipped down the hall to her office. Carol must own every pair of sneakers Marvelous Marley World has ever made. She often showed up in a pair even on formal occasions—the ones with sparkles and spangles.

"I know Dave had trouble before he got to Chicago. His name wasn't always Dave Rollins, either," Teddy Austin said once I'd introduced myself and Carol had put him on the speaker phone.

"What was his name before that?" Carol asked. I slipped her a note with the name, Daniel Devereaux, written on it.

"Wow!" she mouthed the word, rather than interrupting Teddy.

"I can't be sure. When I asked him about it, he said, 'What you don't know can't hurt you. Dave Rollins is my name now and I've got a court decree to prove it. From now on, I do everything by the book.' The way he said it I believed him, and it didn't much matter to me anyway. Dave was Dave."

"Did that 'from now on' part mean he'd had trouble with the law?" I asked. Surely, if he'd had legal problems, Skip would have discovered that, too.

"Could be. Everybody makes mistakes, and whatever happened he seemed to have learned his lesson, so I never asked. It didn't matter to me."

"Well it might matter now since your friend has been murdered," Carol said with a bit of an edge in her voice.

"I heard about it. When Marvelous Marley

World's maestro dies, it's big news."

He was so right! Despite Max's best efforts to keep the lid on the foul play angle, the word was out. In less than forty-eight hours, "Murder of the Maestro" was already "big news," as Dave's old bandmate had said. Retrospectives of his life and career had started to appear with lightning speed on entertainment television news shows.

"That makes me the last living member of our old band. I guess that's what I get for being the runt of the litter. You can probably see that if you have those old photos." What he said was true. Even though Carol had called Dave a scrawny kid, Teddy Austin had been even skinnier.

"We didn't eat much back in those days unless we had a gig at a place that fed us. We made more by eatin' than what they paid us in cash!" Teddy laughed recalling those days.

He rattled on for a couple minutes reminiscing about the places they'd played, their music, and the jazz music scene in Chicago. I enjoyed hearing the stories, but nothing in them appeared to have any bearing on Dave's old troubles or his recent demise.

"I'm sorry Dave's gone. He was a fine man— kind and funny. Generous to a fault. Over the years, he bailed out each one of us old band members at one time or another. What an awful way to go. I wish I could tell you something that would help you figure out who killed him."

"We'll figure it out," I said. "Did Carol already ask you about being part of the memorial event we're planning?"

"Yes, she did. I'm going to come out there for it.

Maybe I'll look up a few people I used to see when I visited more often. If you want to know more about Dave's family, you need to talk to his Aunt Meg. She was the only family member who kept in touch with him back then. When she was in town and we had a gig, she'd come to the club where we were playing. She was a fine-looking woman—black hair and startling gray-green eyes that changed color depending on what she wore. A magnetic personality to go with the gorgeous smile and beautiful face." He paused. "Mm, mm, mm! She was a woman you could never forget. If you really want the scoop about Dave's life before Chicago, ask Aunt Meg."

"I'd love to do that, but I heard she's no longer alive."

"Who said? I got a birthday card from her a few weeks ago from out there where she stays in some place called Mission Viejo." I almost fell off my chair when I heard what he had to say next.

"I don't know exactly where that is since I don't travel much anymore myself and I haven't been to California for years. Dave or that sweet, foxy assistant of his would have told me if Aunt Meg had died."

"You mean Pat?"

"Yeah. I got a birthday card from her, too. It said it was from Dave, but I knew Pat really sent it." Teddy laughed again. "She never let Dave forget his old friends. If something happened to Aunt Meg, I'd know about it."

I was speechless. Fortunately, Carol wasn't. She thanked Teddy. Then she made sure he knew how to contact us about the memorial service or anything having to do with Dave's life in Chicago or California, for that matter. I managed to say goodbye.

After that I got through my meeting with Carol, but I had a hard time concentrating. Pat's puzzling behavior kept intruding into my thoughts. I wasn't the only one who'd figured something odd was going on with Pat. When our meeting ended, Carol asked me a question I could not answer.

"I know Teddy meant it in a different way, but why is Pat being foxy with us about Dave's family and friends?"

13 CATTY CRITICS

All the way home I stewed about Pat. I reran our lunch conversation hoping I could come up with an answer to Carol's question. I'd broached the subject of Dave's past, starting with his Chicago days. Things had gotten off to a good start.

"Wow! The Windy City Jazz Quartet," Pat had said in a soft voice as she sat across from me. "When I first met Dave, he and the members of that group were in frequent contact. Once they all visited for a reunion. They piled into that tiny beach cottage he rented, and I don't think they stopped talking or joking except to play music."

"It sounds as if they were all on good terms."

"Oh, yes, as far as I could tell. Dave hadn't made it big yet, but his career was in lift off. Dave was almost finished with his degree, had made the switch to violin as his instrument of choice. He'd signed on as an intern at Marvelous Marley World, and held court with his old bandmates about the work he was doing with composition, orchestration, and arranging."

"Had he left jazz behind?"

"Not completely, although that's when I first heard someone call him Maestro. They used it as a nickname in place of his old one—the Jazz Man. He still had a bass—an electric bass guitar rather than the huge acoustic stand-up bass he's playing on the cover of the albums the band recorded in Chicago."

"They made records, as in vinyl?"

"Yes. Several albums. They never sold many copies. Dave has a couple of them at the Malibu house and donated others to the Marvelous Marley World archive. It's too bad, though, that once he had enough money to build his big house in Malibu with lots of guestrooms and a high-end home studio, the band never visited again."

"Why not?"

"Dave had settled down. I don't know for sure since Dave and I parted ways for a time. When I started my job as his PA, it was clear to me that Marla would have had a fit if he'd wanted to have a bunch of his old bandmates turn their house into a hotel. The guys in the band had families and careers, too. Barry Midland died the year he turned fifty. That was shortly after I began working for Dave. Dave was so devastated he couldn't even attend the funeral, although he paid for it."

"How did the surviving bandmates take that?"

"I'm not sure, but he remained on speaking terms with the other two men. Teddy Austin came here for a visit not too long ago, but Handley Jones died several years ago."

133

"Do you still know how to reach him?" I had asked. That was the first point at which Pat had turned "foxy" on me, to use Carol's word for it.

"I'm sure I have contact information for him somewhere. I'll look for it."

"If it's easy to find, text it to me, okay? If not, Carol's working on it. I doubt she'll have much trouble tracking him down."

"Sure. He ought to be invited to the memorial event."

"Did Teddy Austin ever say anything about how Dave ended up in Chicago or where he came from?"

"You mean along the lines of Marla's insistence that Dave had a lurid past with women that nearly got him killed?"

"Yes, you sounded as though you believed her when you brought it up on Saturday." Pat hadn't responded right away.

"With Marla, you just never know, do you?"

"She told us she had it on good authority from a relative that Dave was in enough trouble that his family disowned him. Dave's lawyer made it sound worse than that. He says Dave picked the wrong married woman and ended up in the hospital before he took off for Chicago."

"That could be true, but I don't like the idea of airing Dave's dirty laundry. I'm more inclined to believe if Dave's murder has something to do with a woman, it's about the present, not the past. If anyone's vengeful enough to want to punish Dave for his old sins, it's Marla."

"Marla claims you're the most likely person to know about Dave's past sins. Or at least, about any ties he still has to a couple of old family members, his Aunt Meg and a brother named Bill." Pat hadn't made eye contact as she spoke. After speaking to Teddy Austin, I now realized that Pat had come as close to deception as someone could without lying!

"That's possible. When I look for Teddy Austin's number, I'll check." Then she'd changed the subject and we'd moved onto plans for the memorial event. Why had I just let it drop like that? Pat had sounded so matter of fact, not like she was hiding a thing!

"Georgina Shaw, you are going to get to the bottom of this today!" I vowed as I walked into the kitchen. Marched into the kitchen was more like it, and right into a cat ambush. Despite the fact there are only two of them, it felt as if there were cats everywhere! Miles bellowed with Ella echoing her more muted and melodious call. Jumping up onto the side table by the door leading from the garage, they demanded that I pet them. I did as they commanded.

Then they were off to the races, doing this wild rampage through the kitchen, into the great room, up over the back of the couch, under the coffee table, and back into the kitchen.

Normally, their zaniness would have made me laugh out loud. Today it was over the top and made me realize how tired I was after a long day of poking my nose into someone else's life. I felt a little down, too, about the loss of a colleague in a stupid, senseless fashion. Not to mention my inability to get to the bottom of Pat Dolan's dodgy behavior.

"Cool it, will you guys? Let me get a cup of tea before you wreak your havoc, okay?" Miles bellowed in reply. Whether in sympathy or reproach, I couldn't tell, but he wasn't holding a grudge. Cats can do that, as I've learned. Not today. Ella brushed against my legs, chattering sweetly.

Whatever else he'd tried to tell me with that booming communique, curiosity overtook Miles as I set down the items I'd carried in from my car. Miles levitated up onto the side table and sniffed a manila folder full of printed pages Carol had given me. I'd just slipped out of my jacket when Miles' curious sniffing turned into an effort to mark the folder. Despite my appeal for him to cool it, he tilted his head back and issued a Miles Davis like trumpet blast that I bet Teddy Austin would have appreciated.

"Good grief, Miles, Carol's given me stuff to bring home before. What's the problem?" He went at it again—a little more vigorously, and this time knocked the folder onto the floor. In among the printed pages scattered everywhere were photos taken of Dave as he exited the gala. Ella gurgled with delight as she pawed at them. Maybe it was the shiny surface of the glossy photos in the mix that attracted her. She has a passion for anything that glitters, gleams, or sparkles.

"I got the glossies from PR," Carol had explained as she'd shoved the photos into the folder. "They planned to have Dave sign some of them for fans as his last official publicity photos. I doubt they meant that quite so literally, did they?" Carol had asked as she handed me that file folder.

"I'm sure they didn't," I'd replied and sighed then as I did now seeing Dave's smiling face in those photos.

"What part of cool it did you not understand?" I

asked as I tossed my jacket over the back of a barstool freeing both hands to retrieve the photos. Miles and Ella inspected each one in that tenuous way cats do when they're spooked because new items have appeared in their territory or old ones are out of place. I smiled since they appeared to be viewing the photos as I'm sure the folks in PR had done before settling on the ones to be used as publicity shots.

"Everybody's a critic," I said as Ella pawed at one of the glossy pics. Then she grabbed the photo and rolled over onto her back with it. Grasping it in her front paws, she kicked at it with her back ones.

"Give me that, Ella!" She mewed at me in a tone I recognized as unhappy griping. "I'm sorry, but who knows what chemicals could have been used to process that photo? That's not something cats should eat. Treats!" I hollered as I stood and shuffled the stack of photos back into a neat pile.

When I placed the folder on the large granite island in the kitchen, I unwrinkled the one Ella had singled out for special attention. A little tingle ran through me. In it, a stylishly-dressed, attractive young woman stood next to Dave. Her eyes weren't fixed on Dave, though, nor were they looking directly into to the camera. Instead, she gazed at an older woman in the semicircle of smiling people in the photo. I recognized Connie Forsythe immediately. She'd played the starring role in one of Marvelous Marley World's longest running series, *Family Manners*. Connie Forsythe's notoriety hadn't caused the tingling sensation I'd felt. It was the fact that she was wearing one of those diamond brooches Pat had told us about.

"Hmm," I said aloud as I studied that picture trying to make sense of the story it told. "Connie Forsythe's obviously an old flame of Dave's. Why is that young woman so interested in the pin?" I stole a sideways glance at Ella who stood on the barstool beside me with her front paws on the kitchen island peering at that photo once again. Surely that pin wasn't the reason she was displaying such an interest in the photo.

No way, I thought as I leaned in to look more closely at the image. Ella loves shiny objects, but she couldn't have spotted that pin given how small it was. It had to be the glossy, shiny surface of the photo that had attracted her to it. Now, though, not one, but two nosy cats had taken up positions on either side of me. Drawn by my fixed gaze, I suppose, they were taking no chance on missing something. I used a finger to trace the path of the young woman's gaze and it sure seemed like she was fixated on that brooch. The cats' eyes followed the movement of my finger. When I stepped back abruptly, they did too. They didn't abandon their perches on the barstools, but their tails were bushed and switched back and forth.

"Sorry to spook you," I muttered. I'd reacted quickly when it suddenly dawned on me that Pat was in that semicircle, too. Standing there with a pleasant smile on her face. Perhaps she'd observed some interaction between the younger woman and Connie Forsythe as they mingled in that small clutch of partygoers.

"She might at least be able to identify the younger woman. Maybe I can get to the bottom of her evasiveness about Aunt Meg and Bill, while I'm at it," I said grabbing my phone from my bag. I took it with me as I dashed around to the other side of the enormous kitchen island. In a hurry to keep my promise to the cats that treats were coming, I pulled sliced turkey from the fridge, broke it into a few pieces, and dropped it into the kitties' snack bowls. I swear those two Siamese did a double take—looked at me and then at each other before diving off the barstools. Sliced turkey isn't just a treat—it's a super treat.

"Pat, it's Georgie."

"Please don't tell me Max has changed his mind about the venue. I just placed an order to print several thousands of invitations to the memorial service."

"No, it's not that. I have a couple of questions for you about things that came up when Jack and I spoke to Skip and Jennifer. Before that, though, I hope you can help me identify someone from a photo taken at Dave's retirement party. She's a petite blonde with shoulder length hair, blue eyes, and she's wearing a clingy little lacy number that says Oscar de la Renta to me. I'm asking you about her because you're in the photo, too. She's standing between Dave and Connie Forsythe."

"Oh yes, I know who you mean. She's wearing that gorgeous dress with those lovely gold embellishments. That's Connie's niece, Emily Lombard. Why do you ask?"

"One reason is that she's standing next to Dave near the exit at the end of the gala. I wondered if you saw her head out the door with him."

"Not on his arm or anything like that, but I'm pretty sure she was in the group that poured out onto the steps with him as he left. I was swept up in the flow of people all trying to exit and ended up getting pushed back behind him, so I couldn't swear to it."

"The other thing I noticed in the photo is that Connie Forsythe's wearing one of those diamond treble clef pins."

"Yes, I noticed it that night. I'm sure Connie figured it would make Dave happy for her to wear it. She wasn't the only one, by the way."

"Hmm, maybe that's why Emily appears to be gazing at the one her aunt is wearing."

"It's not an embarrassing faux pas like showing up in the same dress, but Emily couldn't have missed the fact Aunt Connie wasn't the only one wearing it. In fact, Connie and Debra Kravitz, the other woman I saw wearing that pin, weren't far from Emily when they whispered something to each other and then had a good laugh about it. I couldn't hear what they said, but I saw Debra point at her own pin as she spoke to Connie and then burst out laughing."

"They're good sports to make light of what could have been a difficult moment," I said.

"They've both been around the block a time or two, and any fling with Dave ended long ago. Connie wasn't always such a good sport, but she eventually came around. I wouldn't be surprised, though, if other women at that gala slipped it into a handbag when they ran into others wearing it, too."

"That would be an unpleasant way to discover you were the member of a club you didn't even know existed, wouldn't it?"

"Unpleasant enough for one of them to follow him home, lure him out to that cliff to give him a shove, and then go back and defile his home, you mean?"

"Something like that," I replied. Or hide in wait for an opportunity to sneak up on him and bash him over the head sending him plunging off the cliff. I kept that possibility to myself since I wasn't sure the police had released the information Jack had shared with me about how the killer had attacked Dave. I didn't have long to think about it when another possibility gripped me. "Did Dave know Emily?"

"Probably. She's been around at entertainment events for years and Connie wasn't shy about promoting her niece's acting career. Emily's had bit parts on *Family Manners* and in other Marvelous Marley World productions. She's a singer too and was hired a couple of years ago as a member of the Marvelous Marley World Merry Minstrels. It's entirely possible Dave's known Emily for years."

"She's young, isn't she?" I tried to imagine how Emily might have reacted if she'd been Dave's guest and he had offered her a pin identical to the one her aunt wore.

"Twenty-something. That's old enough for Dave." Pat paused issuing a big sigh. "Or it would have been since the past tense is more appropriate now, isn't it?"

"Sad, but true. Thanks for the background, Pat. I'll tell Jack about the picture and see if he wants to speak to Emily and her aunt, too, since they're both near Dave as he's leaving the Grand Pavilion."

Especially if Jack's interviews of the valets found out Dave had left the gala in a limo with a lovely young blonde at his side, I added in my head. Even if someone had already identified Emily Lombard by name, Jack would appreciate hearing the backstory Pat had just given me.

"Now that I think about it, I'm almost certain she was tagging along behind him as he headed to the exit. You're right about Connie. She and Debra were both still with him, too, at that point. I don't know what happened once they got outside and headed down the red carpet to the limos."

"Thanks, Pat. Jack's working on it. Maybe he already has a better idea than we do about what happened to Connie and her niece. If not, he'll find this all very interesting." I took a deep breath as I decided to press Pat about the other matter where I needed her help.

"Speaking of aunts and nieces, I have another question for you."

14 RUMORS OF HER DEATH

"When Jack and I met with Jennifer this afternoon, she told us Margaret Landry died recently, but when Carol and I spoke to Teddy a little later, he said he believes she's still alive. He also was very clear that you know how to reach her. Is that true? Do you know her niece, too—Dave's granddaughter, Maggie Knight?"

"Yes." Pat responded. That one word was followed by more silence.

"Why didn't you tell me any of this when we spoke at lunch about contacting Dave's Aunt Meg or his brother?" Pat sighed heavily on the other end of the phone.

"Dave swore me to secrecy. It didn't feel right to bring up any of this even after his death. Besides, it all happened so long ago, Marla's just being a drama queen." Those words tumbled out in a rush. I wasn't going to let the comment about Marla distract me this time. I had other questions I hoped would help me understand what Dave's past life meant in the present.

"Jennifer and Skip seem to believe Maggie Knight's existence came as a complete surprise to Dave."

"Yes. Because he and Meg kept in touch over the years doesn't mean she was open with him. Maybe she was trying to protect Maggie or herself if there was still some danger to them by keeping quiet. I never asked questions about Meg even when Teddy Austin first mentioned her years ago. I communicated with Meg on Dave's behalf from time to time, but I never developed a relationship with her. I hoped to avoid another incident with her like the one I'd had with Marla. As I said, Dave demanded secrecy."

"Maggie Knight's no secret any longer. Jack or another member of the investigative team will interview her since Dave wrote her into his will before he died. That ought to shake things up at the reading of the will." Pat made a little "pshaw" sound on the other end of the phone.

"Despite Dave's secrecy and making me take a vow of silence about Maggie and Meg, Marla must know all about Maggie Knight's existence and what she stands to inherit."

"Whatever she does or doesn't know about Maggie, she told us to contact his brother Bill, or his aunt Meg, to find out more about his past. According to Jennifer and Skip, it's too late to get the story from his Aunt Meg, but Teddy Austin say that's not true. He's adamant that if she'd died you would have told him and says he got a birthday card from her not long ago with a California return address!" My voice increased in volume as I grew more emphatic about my intention to find out what the heck was going on.

"Okay, okay. I surrender. I hope I'm not putting anyone at risk by telling you this. Margaret Landry's not dead. Aunt Meg wasn't Dave's aunt and she's not Maggie's aunt either. She's her grandmother." I was stunned even though it all became as clear as day once Pat said it. My stupefied brain could barely respond.

"Good grief! That did seem like an awful lot of Margarets—too many. I can't believe I didn't make the connection immediately," I babbled. Pat laughed.

"One too many, that's for sure. I know I said I stayed out of Dave's finances, but I should have been more specific. In my role as his PA I've always handled the household budget. When Dave set his up granddaughter in a condo, he moved Margaret Landry into a lovely elder care facility not far from her. The expenses related to Meg's care are paid for from that household account. It's all part of his effort to keep her presence in California a secret. He made me promise not to tell anyone about Meg or Maggie. I assumed it was about avoiding a confrontation with Marla, but after he was killed it seemed even more important not to reveal their whereabouts until the police had figured out who killed Dave. It should have occurred to me sooner that once Dave's lawyers were involved redoing his will, Maggie was no longer a secret from Marla."

"What makes you say that?"

"Marla's lawyer is at the same firm Dave used. For want of a better word, I'll say Marla 'dated' more than one of the firm's partners over the years. I don't believe she relies on pillow talk any more to keep track of Dave's most private business, but she still has her spies."

"How do you know?"

"I don't believe Dave found out, but the witch spoiled his surprise for me. Marla blurted it out in a huff one day, furious that Dave was redoing our little 'love nest' for me. When I asked her what she was talking about, she flew into a snit, telling me not to pretend I didn't know. She claimed she knew for a fact Dave rewrote his will and intended to give the beach cottage to me as a place to retire."

"You never asked Dave if what she said was true?"

"No. Marla took a special delight in telling me she'd spoiled Dave's effort to surprise me. I could never have brought it up without feeling ghoulish about it."

"I understand." Pat and I let out sighs at almost the same time. She spoke next.

"I'll text you the information about how to reach Margaret Landry and Maggie Knight if Jennifer didn't already give it to you. While I'm at it, I'll dig out a phone number I have for his brother Bill, too. Meg and Bill aren't exactly 'next of kin,' but I notified them both about Dave's death. I didn't want them to hear about it from the media. I guess I should have told Jack, huh?"

You could say that again, I thought.

"Yes. Jack will want to speak to them. I'm sure Max will appreciate that you reached out to them."

"I hope so. It's hard to predict how Max will react once he gets the lowdown on who Meg is and how she fits into Dave's life. It's the decent thing to do, and I'm sure she'll be delighted to join us—the rumors of her death having been 'greatly exaggerated,' to borrow a phrase from Mark Twain."

"Max must be used to Dave's scandalous relationships with women by now. Somehow, I doubt Maggie Knight will be a surprise to Max, don't you?"

"That's a good point. Those two were as thick as thieves. When Max's daughter was murdered, he was over here for days at a time. He and Dave holed up for hours in Dave's 'man cave' downstairs. Music blaring and empty scotch bottles, but I'm sure they weren't using the studio to record anything."

"I'll explore this with Max as tactfully as I can. Max may or may not find a new twist on Dave's scandal-ridden life particularly newsworthy, but the press is going to love it. He deserves a 'heads-up' that the news about Maggie Knight is likely to break at any moment. Dave's life as Daniel Devereaux is bound to come out too."

"You're a brave woman. I've never been comfortable with that man, even though he and Dave were so close. Anyway, while I have you on the phone, I've come across a photo that I'd like you and Jack to see. It was in the box of stuff I found near that earring I found. When I went through it again it struck me as interesting given Charlie's claims about an encounter with a wolfman."

"What is it?" I asked.

"It's a photo of Dave and a group of his cronies. It's hard to explain. I want you to decide for yourself if I'm making more out of it than I should. Why don't I drop it off on my way home from errands I'm running and let you two judge it for yourselves? I can get to your house in twenty minutes, if that's okay."

"Of course, it's okay. While you're here, you can peek at the one I called you about and see if I've missed anything interesting. I'll leave your name at the guardhouse, so they'll let you in. Jack should be here by then, and he can look at it, too. Do you want to join us for dinner?"

"No. I have a dinner date already, and I won't be able to stay long," she replied. There was a pleasant lilt to her voice that gave me the impression it really was a date.

Pat's just full of surprises today," I thought as I thanked her and then ended our call. I like Pat and felt relieved that we'd cleared the air about her reticence to share important details of Dave's life—even after he was brutally murdered. She had gone straight to Jack with that earring she'd found and was doing the same with a photo that could have something to do with Charlie's wolfman.

"She's right that I'll have to see it to believe it," I murmured in anticipation.

15 THE WOLF GANG

I was still pondering Pat's latest revelations when I heard the automatic garage door open. Miles and Ella, who had been lazily grooming themselves after their windfall of turkey treats, went on alert. Even before my conversation with Pat, I'd been anxious to hear what Jack had to say about progress with the investigation.

Now, I had plenty to tell him, too. After sharing Jack Wheeler's life for a year, I'd discovered that table talk about murder and mayhem was a regular occurrence. It still struck me as odd, at times. Today, though, I was so determined to find out who killed Dave Rollins I was going to introduce the topic of murder even before we sat down to eat.

"What a waste," I muttered. Who knew what other contributions Dave could have made even in retirement if he'd lived longer? The maestro had his faults, especially when it came to compulsive womanizing, but he'd been a talented composer and gifted musician. A generous man, too, as Teddy

Austin said. I'd always known that, but I'd come to understand how generous after speaking to Jennifer and Skip. Dave would get the justice he deserved if I had anything to say or to do about it!

I stepped out from behind the island in the kitchen and grabbed my coat from the barstool. The cats swiveled their heads toward me, and then back toward the sound coming from the garage. Miles hadn't quite adjusted to the fact that he now had two humans to keep tabs on. Ella, who's much younger than Miles, follows his lead whenever they're confronted by an ambiguous situation.

"You guys stay put. I'll be right back," I said as I dashed down the hall to change out of the pantsuit I'd worn to work. I didn't hear the pitter-patter of little cat feet, so they must have understood me. Not that I was deluded enough to believe they did so out of obedience. Cats have no bosses.

As I changed clothes, I decided that with Pat on her way to the house, we might as well put dinner on hold. Chicken Marsala was on the menu. The dish is deceptively simple and quick, despite the hoity-toity sounding name. I'd saved a step, too, by buying chicken the butcher had already pounded into thin slices. The chicken would cook in a flash, and so would the fresh linguini I'd bought to accompany the chicken.

Cheese with fruit and crackers would hold us over until we'd finished our business with Pat. That would make Jack happy, too, since our snack could pass as dessert. He's an "eat dessert first" kind of guy, as I discovered early in our relationship. A very practical approach for a man who loves dessert as much he does and leads an unpredictable life as a police detective.

"Hello, Doll," Jack said when I hurried back into the kitchen. Little Ella was in his arms and I could hear her purring from across the room. When he put her down, both cats, tails pointing skyward, followed him into the kitchen as he greeted me with a hug. "What's cooking?"

"Nothing right now," I replied and quickly filled him in on my phone call with Pat and her impending visit, telling him how helpful Teddy Austin had been in helping me get to the truth about Meg Landry. As I spoke, I cut wedges of creamy brie and put them onto small plates. I drizzled them with honey and then topped them with a small handful of almonds. With crackers, apple slices, and grapes, Jack and I ought to be able to hold out for dinner until we'd concluded our business with Pat.

"She has turned out to be pivotal to this investigation, hasn't she?" As he asked that question, Jack removed the jacket to what I call his "detective's uniform." He hung it up and slipped on a weathered fleece jacket instead. I've offered to help him upgrade his wardrobe, but he's refused. Jack's not a fan of shopping and doesn't want to do anything to trigger more ribbing about "marrying money."

It's true I make more money than he does, but my brothers and I had been gifted with a rich inheritance from our hardworking, loving parents that hadn't included money. Not like Dave's kids, his ex-wife Marla, and granddaughter Maggie Knight. Pat, too, as we'd learned. I hoped the prospect of getting their hands on all that money hadn't been a motive for murder.

"It's too bad Pat didn't give you a heads-up sooner about Dave's secrets."

"Better late than never," Jack said as I opened the sliders to the veranda and he carried our plates to the table. "Withholding information isn't exactly lying. I can understand how Dave's death could have confused her about where to place her loyalties. At least she's getting that photo to us quickly." I dialed up the outside lights now that the sun had almost slipped below the horizon. The evening air was chilly, and I switched on the heater in the patio cover. I couldn't entirely blame my chills on the weather, though. A conversation about murder adds a different kind of chill to the air.

"I have a photo to share with you, too. Carol found this one." With that, I darted back into the house and retrieved that folder that held the photos of Dave at his retirement gala.

When I returned, I handed the folder to Jack and sat down beside him. As he flipped through the contents, I caught sight of that telltale piece of jewelry Connie Forsythe wore standing next to her niece, Emily Lombard. I stopped Jack.

"This is the picture I wanted to show you. Ella found it fascinating," I said, smoothing it again.

"Tasty, too, if those fang marks are any indication," Jack quipped.

"You know how fond she is of shiny things. I figured the gloss on this photo attracted her. She started to work it over before I could snatch it away."

"At least she didn't steal it." Ella not only has a fondness for shiny things, but a propensity to claim them and squirrel them away to play with later.

"I'm wise to our little cat burglar who has a 'tell'—a special gurgle when she's found a priceless treasure. Anyway, once I retrieved it from her, I recognized Connie Forsythe right away. Pat's standing nearby so I called her and asked her if she could remember the younger woman next to Connie. The one who appears fixated on that pin Connie's wearing. See?" I explained that the younger woman was Connie's niece, filled him in on what Pat and I suspected about her fascination with Connie's pin, and Pat's recollection that both women were swept outside with Dave as he left the gala.

"That's interesting. Pat hasn't seen this yet, has she?"

"No, but I'm sure she's correct. Also, I didn't notice it the first time, but check out the woman standing off to the side behind Emily. Does that earring look familiar to you?" Jack sat up straighter in his chair.

"It sure does, doesn't it?"

"Have you heard anything from the lab investigators about it?"

"Nothing yet. If we're lucky, they might be able to get DNA from it. Hank asked them to make it a priority, but that won't happen overnight even if they expedite the process. It's one of the few pieces of evidence from the crime scene that could be used to place a specific woman at his house that night. What do you want to bet we've found the owner of that missing earring?"

"I'm not a betting woman, but I'd say it's no coincidence. It's too bad we can't see her face."

"Carol must have other photos from the gala. Do you think she can find one where the woman's face is visible?"

"I'll ask. Maybe Pat can tell us who it is. The woman must have been milling about in the crowd of people surrounding Dave. If Pat bumped into her, maybe she can remember who she is." Just then, the doorbell rang.

"Stay put. I'll get it!" When Jack returned moments later, Pat was with him. Two curious Siamese cats trailed behind them. When Jack and Pat joined me on the veranda, Miles and Ella settled down into Sphinx-like poses inside. My hunch about her dinner appointment being a date was correct, judging by her appearance. She was stunning in the pricy little black dress she wore. Her hair and makeup were flawless, too.

"You look gorgeous!" I exclaimed. That got a big smile from Pat.

"I do clean up nicely, don't I?" She was beaming. "I only have a few minutes. Maybe this doesn't mean anything, but when I saw it I thought Charlie might not be as off base as he sounded about his wolfman claim."

Pat placed a photo on the table near the file folder Carol had given me. In the photo Dave and several other people were all dressed in period outfits with one notable exception in their garb. What struck me immediately, was a sea of white hair. Not a gathering of elders with snowy white hair like Santa or Max Marley, but a group of men sporting powdered wigs. Had the wolfman been wearing one under his hoodie?

In addition to his wig, Dave was adorned in a long, gold brocade frock coat, a pair of black knee breeches, a black vest with an attached jabot, and a pair of cuffs. Dave and a couple of the other fellows had opened their jackets and vests to reveal a popular modern-day undergarment—a t-shirt. Bold gold letters stood out against a black background: Wolf Gang.

"Where was this taken?" I asked.

"When?" Jack added.

"I'm almost certain Dave and his pals are in a room at the City Club. Dave belonged to the club for years, so I'm not sure I can pinpoint a date for you, Jack. It's well before they moved the club to LA's Financial District. That's where you'll have to go to track someone down who might be able to help you determine when this event took place."

"Did Dave ever tell you anything about the Wolf Gang. Do you recognize anyone with him in this photo?" Jack asked.

"I thought you might ask me that. Yes, I believe he mentioned the Wolf Gang, but only in passing. Honestly, I can't even recall what he said except that it had something to do with the time he spent in music school. The two I've seen before are Dave's friends from his college days at USC. The tall one with the infectious grin, is James Bellagio. The last I heard, he was teaching music at Vanderbilt. A real prankster as I recall. Next to him is Gerald Pratt who's no longer with us. That older man behind Dave is the professor who mentored him at USC—Dr. Francis Kendall. I looked him up. He died, too, in 1997 so that'll give you an even better idea of how old this picture must be."

"That doesn't leave us with many options when it comes to finding out more about the Wolf Gang, does it?"

"I'm afraid not. I went through that box of stuff hoping I'd find more information about the group, but no luck. That's odd because I'm sure there was more in there. It didn't mean much to me before now, but Dave was pawing through it a couple of weeks ago. When I asked what he was doing he said someone wanted him to create a Mozart fan club to mentor talented high school musicians. He hoped to get members from an old group involved. He didn't call it the Wolf Gang and I let it go without asking more questions, although I glimpsed this picture, or one like it among the items on his desk. I'm sure the Wolf Gang must be what they were referring to as the Mozart fan club."

"No red t-shirt, either, like Charlie claimed the guy he spoke to was wearing."

"Maybe the group members had more than one version of their shirts," Pat suggested. "The Wolf Gang must have been active during the period in which Dave and I had gone our separate ways."

"There are a couple of young men in this photo." I stared at the faces of two young men dressed in different outfits.

"Yes. The two guys standing by the door like footmen might only be in their twenties," Jack commented. "They're not sporting tees of any color." Jack handed that photo to Pat.

"They look like servers hired to wait on the Wolf Gang members to me. If you take this with you to the club, someone might be able to answer that question for you," she said placing the photo back on the table.

"First, too many Margarets and now, too many Mozarts," I muttered. Jack and Pat both stared at me. "Oh, you know what I mean. I thought there were three women named Margaret in Dave's life when there really are only two. What I'm talking about now is not just all these guys dressed like Mozart, but all the encounters with Mozart—presuming the t-shirt Charlie saw said Wolf Gang not wolfman. It can't be a coincidence given the fact that whoever broke into Dave's home took the time to mess with items related to the now defunct Wolf Gang. Skip also mentioned that Dave had been harassed by some crazed Mozart fan, right?"

"He received notes, off and on, from that character for years. Nothing recent." Her eyes widened. "I never made any connection between the Wolf Gang and the writer of those notes. Maybe Dave did, because I'm sure they were in that box, too. They're gone now."

"Did the writing in those notes look like the same script used in the lettering on the banner and t-shirts in these photos?"

"Not identical," she responded after peering at the photo. "Darn close, though. I never asked Dave about a link between the notes and the Wolf Gang. He was so odd about those incidents. Sometimes he laughed at the content of the notes. At other times, he seemed troubled and got edgy if I urged him to send them to his legal team."

"Maybe he knew who was behind them all along and that's why he wouldn't take legal action," I suggested.

"Another of Dave's many secrets, if that's the case. One he didn't share with me. Those letters don't have any cash value. Should I report the fact that they're missing to the Lost Hills police department?"

"Yes. Do that tomorrow so they get into the official record. I'll give Hank Bardot a call and tell him about the missing letters and the Wolf Gang, so he doesn't blow you off when you call. All this wolfman stuff is out there."

"Not too far out there if it's tied to a delusional fan who wanted to destroy Dave and his work. He wouldn't be the first celebrity to face something like that."

"While we're pondering Mozart-related incidents, I have another one for you. Do you remember Hank telling us the vandal had left a little night music blaring from Dave's house?" Pat and I both nodded our heads yes. "At the time, I thought he was referring to the Broadway musical or trying to be flippant about the neighbors' complaints. As it turns out, the loud music was a jazz recording Dave had made." Jack paused. I held my breath waiting to hear the punch line.

"When Hank said *A Little Night Music*, he meant a piece Mozart wrote that Dave and his friends performed years ago in a jazz tribute to the classic composer." Pat must have been holding her breath, too, because we both responded with audible gasps.

"I know the track well. It was on a *Mozart Meets Jazz* album. The whole album combined jazz with classical music honoring his jazz roots and his training in music school at USC."

"Does that mean his bandmates in the Windy City Jazz Quartet performed on the recording?"

"Yes, along with a couple of his college pals, so maybe a member or two of the Wolf Gang." Pat glanced at her watch. "Shoot! This is fascinating, but I've got to run. If I remember anything else, I'll call you, Georgie." I stood up to walk with her to the front door.

"You've been a big help already," Jack added. I studied his face wondering if Pat's visit had set to rest his earlier concerns that she'd been holding out on us.

"There sure are plenty of puzzle pieces about Mozart, but they don't seem to fit together, do they? And then there are the women...so many women." When Pat said that about the women, I suddenly remembered the women in the photo Carol had found.

"Hang on, Pat. Can you take a quick look at this photo I told you about?" I slid the picture out of the folder.

"No doubt about it, that's Connie and her niece Emily, just minutes before Dave left the building."

"What about this one?" I asked pointing to the woman wearing the gold earring.

"That sure looks like the earring, but I can't tell who's wearing it from this angle. I can't even see her dress. Unlike those pins the maestro handed out, the earrings weren't very distinctive or memorable. I'm sorry." Pat shrugged and apologized again as I walked her to the door. "You could be on the right track. You won't give up, will you?"

"No," I said, as my mind whirred with plans. Pat's visit had energized and intrigued me. I wanted

Carol to find me more photos of the woman wearing the earrings. I also wanted to speak to Teddy Austin again about what went on during the production of that *Mozart Meets Jazz* recording. And, I planned to call Maggie Knight and invite myself over for a visit with Margaret Landry. When I returned to the kitchen, I proclaimed my renewed determination to find Dave's killer.

"I'm on a crusade until this case is solved. Men aren't the only ones who can be knights in shining armor. Take Joan of Arc, for example," I asserted swishing the air with an imaginary sword.

"On my honor as a knight, I'll be there every step of the way, St. Georgie of Crystal Cove," Jack said bowing from the waist and then kissing my hand! "Promise me if I'm not at your side, you won't do anything that's going to get you burned at the stake or harmed in any other way, okay?" I gulped.

"That is how St. Joan ended up, isn't it?" I gave my worried knight a reassuring peck on the cheek. "I'm not any more interested in ending up as kindling for a bonfire than I was in being buried under a pile of rocks and dirt. You must know by now that I'm tough as rock on the outside to protect the chicken that dwells within. Speaking of chicken, let's go fix dinner."

"Is it Chicken Marsala with those creamy mashed potatoes?"

"Linguini, tonight. I won't deprive you of your favorite mashed potatoes, though. I'm using them as a topping for Shepherd's Pie with a pastry crust. I'll need your expert opinion on whether it makes the cut as a new menu item for the *Arielle's Cottage* restaurant in Arcadia Park."

"I'll do my best, but it could take more than one pie to make a decision like that without a rush to judgement." Jack grinned. He's almost as big a fan of Shepherd's Pie as he is of dessert pies.

"I wouldn't expect any less of the legendary lawman Max regards so highly."

"Please, let's not spoil my appetite by bringing him up. That you hold me in high regard is all that I ask, St. Joan." I pulled him close and did my wifely best to show him a little of the regard I hold for him. Not all that saintly, but what the heck?

The Chicken Marsala was delicious. I would have enjoyed it more if the flattened pieces of chicken hadn't reminded me of our close call on the stairway to Dave's cliff house. After dinner, Jack and I settled into the great room with decaf coffee making notes about all the discoveries of the day.

The blessed quiet in which Jack and I tackled our tasks was suddenly interrupted. First, by a trumpet blast from mighty mouth Miles, only seconds before Jack's phone rang. Deep in thought when our domestic bliss screeched to an end, he took off to retrieve his phone from where he'd left it on the kitchen island. Jack had rolled up his sleeves to help me prepare dinner having become quite adept at assisting me in the kitchen. I hoped I'd learn to be as much help to him in my apprenticeship as a sleuth. When he returned, it was easy to see he had news and it wasn't good.

"What's up? Do I want to know?" Jack's expression told me the answer to that question was a big, fat, "no!"

16 A SAD REPRISE

"Charlie's dead," Jack replied. "The first responders say there was drug paraphernalia at the scene. If he died from an accidental overdose, I'll give up dessert for a month." I jumped to my feet. Cats flew in opposite directions.

"Why Charlie?"

"I don't know. Maybe the wolfman didn't want Charlie talking to the police. That's too bad because I hoped if we showed Charlie that picture he could tell us if Wolf Gang was what was written on the red t-shirt, or if the wolfman's white hair looked like one of those wigs," Jack responded.

"Charlie had already spoken to the police. Why kill him now?" I asked.

"Charlie wasn't the best witness, I'll give you that. Still, the wolfman may have reached a different conclusion about Charlie's value to us."

"I suppose if you ever managed to track the guy down, Charlie might have been able to identify him."

"He was more than willing to try. Talking to the police could have been enough for the killer to be out for blood even if he had nothing to gain."

"Any progress figuring out how the wolfman knew we were going to be on those stairs Sunday?"

"We're still putting together a timeline from the round robin of interviews with all the people at Dave's estate when we were attacked." Jack chewed his bottom lip—a sure sign my husband was unhappy about the information he'd just shared with me.

"Come on, Detective. What's the rest of the story?"

"I'm not sure how much more progress we *can* make on that front. Everyone heard we were on our way. I don't care how much time we spend trying to piece together who was where when, there were just too many people at that house to be sure about their whereabouts. With so many people doing tasks in different locations, we may not be able to figure out who disappeared long enough to try to kill us or scare us off."

"It didn't work." I added, shrugging since I couldn't see what difference scaring us off would have made anyway.

"I know, but it did delay our arrival. Maybe that was the intention."

"Why bother with us?"

"Not us. *You*, Georgie. I don't have any history with Dave Rollins, but you do."

"Me? I've told you what kind of history I've had with Dave. Our relationship was strictly collegial and not even as close as those I've had with lots of other coworkers."

"If this is about payback for Dave's indiscretions with women, maybe the wolfman doesn't know that. Or one of the women you've spoken to the past couple of days didn't believe you and sicced the wolfman on us to punish you."

"Who? You can't mean Pat, can you? She couldn't care less about the other women in Dave's life. If I didn't believe it before today, I do now." Jack stood there staring at me. Clueless. "Wasn't it obvious by the spring in her step? The makeup, hair, and dress? Pat was on her way to a romantic rendezvous. She's not holding the torch for Dave or a grudge if there's someone waiting who can put a spark like that into a dinner date."

"She was wearing a nice fragrance." Jack still didn't appear to be completely convinced. He moved on anyway. "What about Marla?"

"Marla might send an assassin after me if I stood to inherit money from Dave. I wouldn't trust her completely even if I were one of her kids. Maybe there's an old score to be settled at Marvelous Marley World and it's a matter of guilt by association since I'm in management."

"I hadn't considered the workplace angle. You can check it out if you'd like, but if this is about an old workplace dispute, that could potentially involve lots more people. That's all we need. We not only have too many Margarets and too many Mozarts, but way too many people altogether, don't we? I'd like to believe this loosey goosey wolfman Charlie met is behind all the recent incidents, but we don't have a lick of evidence tying him to Dave Rollins' murder. We can't be sure the wolfman and the Mozartobsessed fan who hassled Dave are one and the same, nor do we know without any doubt he's the man with a bucket of rocks. Besides, who knows how much we can trust the word of a down and out guy like Charlie? Charlie had a police record."

"For drugs?" I asked. "Charlie's police record—was it for drug-related offenses?"

"No. Panhandling, loitering, and public nuisance complaints. Minor offenses, like that but lots of them. That's a clear indication to me of a guy who was unwilling or unable to learn from his mistakes." Jack shook his head.

"If he was picked up that many times, he couldn't have kept his involvement in drugs hidden."

"That's one reason I doubt his death was an accident." Jack sighed heavily. He lumbered after me, brooding, as I picked up our coffee cups and carried them into the kitchen.

"Let's hope we get a break once the CSIs have gone over the spot where Charlie's body was found. They're on the way now. Hank also has Tony and his other officers working overtime running background checks on everyone at Dave's house on Sunday. He didn't like it when I added more names for them to check, but I want them to check up on the Wolf Gang members we've identified so far. Tomorrow I'm going to see what I can find out by visiting City Club."

"You do have your hands full, Detective Wheeler. I'm sure this case isn't the only one in your portfolio of misdeeds, either. Why don't I take a first crack at talking to the women while you continue to chase down the potential bad guys?"

"What did I just say about you being a person of interest to the wolfman or whoever has sent him after you if he's not acting on his own?"

"I don't mind being in protective custody while you're around, darling." I gave my worried husband a hug. "You can't afford to babysit me 24/7. Besides, I'm a working woman and I've got mysteries to solve, too. It's true the biggest one right now involves cake." Jack said nothing as I stepped around to a cupboard where I'd stashed a takeout box. "Carol and I are meeting with the caterers to decide what to serve at the company memorial for Dave. I'd appreciate your help on my desperate dilemma. I brought samples home."

"Is there no end to the demands of married life?" He asked. "It'll have to be quick. I'm going to have to leave you unsupervised sooner than either of us would like." I paused before the tiny sliver of cake I was transferring from the box reached the plate I'd placed in front of Jack.

"Uh-oh," was all I could come up with reading the look in Jack's eyes.

"Dave Rollins' murder was outside my jurisdiction. They found Charlie's body on a beach closer to home."

"How close?" I asked as my wifely intuition told me there was more to what he was saying.

"At the northern end of Crystal Cove, a few miles up the road from here." I sucked in a breath.

"That's another message, isn't it?" I asked and quickly set out the remaining cake samples for Jack.

"Maybe. It's another reason to be careful." In too short a time, Jack had picked his favorites.

"It's likely to be a late night. Don't wait up, okay?" I nodded, although I might as well wait up. No way was I going to sleep until he got home anyway. Once Jack had slipped back on his Detective Wheeler suit jacket, he gave me a kiss and then dashed toward the door leading out into the garage. Ella cut him off, crossing his path at a diagonal, from his right. Jack stopped, bent down and patted her.

"I'll be back. Keep Mama company while I'm gone, okay?" She blinked at him with her stunning blue eyes. When batting her eyes at him like that didn't work, and Jack took another step, she cut him off again. This time she got assistance from Miles who let out a mournful cry. In one fell swoop, Jack picked up both cats and deposited them on barstools at the kitchen island. "Treats!" He exclaimed. The cats looked at me expectantly.

"That won't work. They know it's too early for more treats." Steely-eyed, their gazes didn't waver as Jack gave me a wink and slipped out the door. "Oh, okay. More treats it is, you spoiled kitties."

17 COOKIE INTERROGATION

It was a restless night. Much of it spent in that twilight zone, not fully asleep or awake. My dreams were filled with images of people with powdery white bouffant hairdos. Some of them hung on the wall in ornate frames. Like a scene from one of Max Marley's ghost story films—*Witch Hazel's Haunted Warren* or *Spirits of Wildflower Hollow*. It wasn't until Jack slipped into bed that I fell deep asleep. By the way I felt, and he looked, we were both in for a rugged day.

"What time did you get in last night?" I asked as I pulled coffee cups from the cupboard and filled one for my groggy husband and another for me.

"This morning you mean? It was after one o'clock. No more bodies at the beach, for a while, I hope. Tide and time wait for no man and with a steady breeze blowing in, I could add wind to that adage. There was a big push to document the scene and clean up before nature could take its course and damage the evidence."

"Another body that might have vanished if someone hadn't phoned in that tip." I was speaking to myself as I leaned over and set Jack's coffee in front of him. Jack responded as if I'd spoken to him. I sipped my coffee, relishing the boost the steamy brew gave me.

"Correct. Charlie's body was closer to the water and without a bunch of rocks to block the wave action. I left a message for my colleagues to do what they can to find out where that call came from last night. If we're lucky we'll get a lead on the caller, but I'm not holding my breath. We'll have to wait for the coroner's report before we know for certain what killed Charlie. The CSIs don't believe Charlie was killed where we found him. That's another reason they were so keen to preserve his body and comb the area for anything in the vicinity that could give us a clue about where he was killed."

"Or whodunit," I added. I jumped a little when that comment was punctuated by the pinging of the toaster.

"That would be nice to learn, too, before someone else gets murdered." A worried expression stole over Jack's weary face. He sighed loudly as I handed him a toasted bagel with cream cheese and smoked salmon. Miles and Ella went on alert. Both cats tilted their heads back sniffing the air, followed by a volley of enthusiastic vocalizations. They floated up onto the barstools on either side of Jack and he visibly relaxed as they purred loudly.

"Don't let them con you into believing they need to be fed. They already scarfed down their morning treats while you were in the shower. If you give in and feed their fish addiction, it won't be good for them. Lox have too much sodium for cats." Just as I got those words out, Ella reached out and tried to pull Jack's arm toward her, peering up at him with her big baby blues.

"Aw, look how much she loves me. Sorry, little girl. Mama says no." Both cats looked straight at me. It broke my heart a little, but I didn't yield. "I'll bet your doting cat mama has something else special tucked away in the fridge just for the two of you. Right?" Jack asked, adding his now twinkling eyes to the stare down I faced.

"This is getting to be a very bad habit. Treats! More treats, you rascals." I dug out a slice of turkey, broke it into bits, and dropped the pieces into their treat bowls. The cats were already at my feet, having flown from the barstools when they heard their favorite word. "Turkey addicts, too! Speaking of addictions, did Charlie die from a drug overdose?"

"On the face of it." Jack winced. "I won't go into the unsavory details over breakfast, but let's just say someone tried to make it appear as if he died while using drugs. Totally staged. Pointless, too, since he'd also been hit on the back of the head." I sucked in an audible gulp of air—loud enough that Miles and Ella stopped pigging out and glanced up at me. Only for a moment, however, before they resumed wolfing down turkey bits as though they were starving.

"Hit on the head just like Dave?"

"Not the same weapon, but the method's similar. An angry impulsive act."

"It was no small feat to move a dead man from one place to another. If it's the same culprit who threw rocks at us, why not scream and run away like he did that day? Why take the extra risk of securing drugs to set the scene?"

"Those are great questions. The killer might have had no choice but to move Charlie if the location of his murder would have given away the killer's identity." Jack finished his breakfast and emptied his coffee cup. "Still, a clever killer would have dumped the body where it might never have been found rather than set up that hokey drug overdose situation."

"Whoever it is isn't all there—not all the time anyway. Maybe the drugs belong to the killer and the impulsiveness is tied to getting high."

"That's as good an explanation as any. It doesn't make me feel any better about the killer's decision to choose a dump site this close to where we live." Worry was on his face again. "Take Carol with you if you visit the Margarets or go talk to Connie Forsythe or her niece, okay?" My mouth popped open.

"You told me you were going to interrogate the women in your crusader role. Not that they'll necessarily realize that's what you're up to since you'll most likely drop in with cake or cookies!" Jack added, tilting his head back and bobbing his head as he sniffed the air just like those cats had done minutes earlier. "Which is it? I smelled dessert the minute I walked into the house at one a.m. If I hadn't been exhausted, I would have conducted a thorough investigation and uncovered the concealed goods."

"Cookies. What was I supposed to do to keep from worrying about my detective husband while he's at a gruesome crime scene until late at night? I baked like a maniac! Your dessert's ready for this evening.

Since I got so carried away, your idea about using them to ply the truth from unsuspecting suspects is a great one. Cookie interrogation might just work."

"My idea, huh? You're not going to try out my innovation in investigative techniques without having me taste-test your secret weapon, are you?"

"You're as big a con artist as those cats," I harrumphed, caving in immediately. "Oatmeal chocolate chip cookies aren't that bad for breakfast."

"Oh, heck no! Chocolate's heart healthy as you've taught me. You're the perfect wife for an 'eat dessert first' guy like me." Jack was laying it on thick.

"Aw, a wee bit of the blarney already this fine morning. What woman could resist a compliment like that one? How about a refill on your coffee to go with the cookies?" Jack nodded with the expectant look of a ten-year-old on his handsome face.

I laughed as I opened one of several plastic containers filled with cookies and placed a couple on a plate for Jack. The aroma of chocolate, spices, and sugar filled the air. I resisted the urge to do the head-bobbing Jack and the cats had done but failed to pass up a cookie.

"Yum!" Jack said once he'd downed a bite of cookie with a gulp of coffee. "What else have you got in those cookie boxes?" He eyed the stack I'd pulled out from a storage cabinet.

"You'll find out soon enough. Not until lunchtime at your office, I hope. This box is for you to take with you to work. I don't know how you and your colleagues do what you do every day. You can add cookie therapy to cookie interrogation as your wife's innovations in investigative procedures."

"You're a clever sleuth. Not just because of the cookies, either. People trust you, as they should. I hope that means you have better luck than we have locating Emily Lombard. She's not at her condo and her aunt Connie claims she doesn't have a clue where she is, but suggested we contact her parents in Fresno. That didn't work, either."

The more Jack spoke, the more anxious I became about the young woman in that photo. I remembered the conversation Jack and I had about the reasons the woman with Dave the night hadn't come forward.

"Are you saying no one has seen or heard from her since Friday night when she was at that gala?"

"No, I'm not saying that. No one's reported her as a missing person. Neither her aunt nor her parents were as worried about her as you are at this moment. That tells me they know where she is but aren't willing to help us locate her."

"That's more than a little suspicious if you're right."

"I could always be wrong, but yes, I'm more than a little suspicious. Good luck tracking her down. If anyone can do it, though, you can. Even with your faithful companion Carol at your side, promise you'll be extra careful until we have this mess sorted out."

"I will if you will." The three-fingered Boy Scout salute was my reply. Coffee and sugar had worked wonders. Jack was humming as he left the house.

I felt enormous relief at how sure he was that Emily Lombard hadn't become a third victim of the person or persons who'd killed Dave and Charlie. I could be wrong too, but I couldn't picture Emily Lombard as Dave's ruthless killer. Nor could I come up with any reason for her to want to murder poor Charlie.

Jack was right about one thing. I couldn't wait to interrogate the women in Dave's life. I wasn't even going to wait until I got to work to try that phone number I had for Maggie Knight. It wasn't even eight yet, so I showered and dressed. Then, I called her hoping to set up a time to meet today or tomorrow. Those cookies wouldn't stay fresh forever, nor would they hang around for long with a chocoholic like me and an eat dessert first guy in the house.

"Maggie Knight speaking." The voice that responded to my call was a pleasant one. I quickly apologized for calling before nine, explained who I was, and expressed my condolences for the loss of her grandfather. Before she could say much more than a tentative "thank you," I continued speaking and made my pitch.

"We're organizing an event at Marvelous Marley World to memorialize your grandfather's life and work. Max Marley has asked us to make sure Dave's closest friends and his family have a chance to give us input about how best to do that. I'd love to include you and your grandmother, Meg Landry, in the process if you're willing to meet with me. I don't mind doing that wherever it's most comfortable and convenient for you and your grandmother." After that bout of speed-talking, I shut up and took in a deep breath—holding it for what seemed like forever—until Maggie responded.

"This is kind of a tough time for both of us. My grandmother and I are still in shock. I barely had a chance to get to know him and he's gone. It's hard on grandma, too. After so many years learning to live without him, she lets him back into her life and suddenly he's gone again." Maggie sighed deeply. I thought I was going to lose her when she finally spoke again. "We need to meet soon though, don't we?"

"If possible," I replied, buoyed by the fact that she hadn't told me to go away.

"I'm taking Grandma out this morning for a doctor visit. Then she has a hair appointment. I promised her lunch somewhere with a view of the ocean after that. Can you meet us for lunch or dessert?"

"I'd be happy to do that. Just say where and when."

"Um, that's a problem since I don't exactly know how long her morning appointments will take. You know they can keep you waiting at the doctor's office? We're winging it at the salon, too. If you have a suggestion for a place she'd enjoy eating, I'd appreciate that, too. It'll be tough to make a reservation, though, won't it?" Maggie Knight sighed. "Maybe we should try later in the week. It can't be tomorrow because I'm tied up all day. Let me pull up my calendar on my phone and check."

I could feel the opportunity to speak to the two Margarets slipping away. Then two words popped into my head in big, bright letters: views and dessert. I had both.

"How about this? Why not have lunch with me at my house?" I explained where I lived and that the ocean views would be distant ones, but we wouldn't need a reservation.

"Grandma would love it. Are you sure it's not too much bother on such short notice?" Truthfully, I would have to hustle to make this work. Who knew what Carol would have to do to join us? I wanted her in the loop not just because I'd promised Jack to take her with me, but because she was handling so many of the details related to the memorial service for Dave. Still, it seemed like my best chance to corner these two women for a solid round of cookie interrogation. A homier, more private setting might make it easier to have the discussion I also hoped to have with them about Dave's past.

"It's no trouble at all," I replied, crossing my fingers as I told that fib. "Let's aim for lunch around one-thirty. Give me a ring if it's going to be later than that."

"Thanks so much. This is such a relief. Grandma won't admit it, but she has trouble hearing in noisy places like crowded restaurants." Miles, who had been stretched out next to Ella in a pool of sunshine, decided to pick that moment to roar like the mini-lion that he is at heart.

"Hush, Miles. Sorry," I said. "It's not always quiet around here. I hope you and your grandmother are okay with cats. I should have mentioned that in case either of you have allergies. Not just to cats, but to particular foods."

"We love cats. Neither of us can have them where we're living. My housing situation is about to change and one of the first things I'm going to do is get a kitten. Maybe two!" The joy that prospect offered was apparent in her voice. Her entire mood picked up. "Wait until I tell Grandma—lunch with a view and cats. No food allergies, either. We grew up in Southern Louisiana where even if you had them you wouldn't admit it. Food is a big deal and you don't want to miss out on something delicious just because it might not agree with you." When she mentioned Southern Louisiana, I could hear just a hint of an accent. A soft laugh followed, like the sound of piano keys being struck perfectly. I was going to enjoy meeting the two Margarets.

"What are some of your grandma's favorite dishes?" Maggie's enthusiasm for adventurous eating was contagious.

"Any kind of seafood—especially fish with meuniere sauce."

"Isn't that interesting? Sole Meunière was one of your grandfather's favorites, too. We've included it on the menu at a Marvelous Marley World event more than once because he requested it."

"Yes, my grandmother and grandfather really were soulmates. It's too bad life got in the way of their happiness." Her tone had turned wistful and a pause followed. Not a long one this time. "Please don't go to any extra trouble. Whatever you're planning for your lunch will be fine with us. It's kind of you to invite us to your home. We'll see you and Miles this afternoon."

The instant I said goodbye to Maggie Knight, I called Carol. As I waited for her to pick up the phone, I inventoried the pantry. I had everything I needed to fix Margaret Landry her favorite dish except for the fish. I knew exactly where I could get it on my way back home.

Should I take the morning off and forget going into my office at all? I wondered. A second later, I got my answer to that question.

"Georgie, I was just about to call you." There was an intensity in Carol's voice. Had the news been released about poor dead Charlie Daniels? That was fast.

"I take it you heard the news."

"What news?"

"Charlie Daniels was killed last night. Murdered and his body left on the beach near Crystal Cove."

"Yikes! I hadn't heard, but maybe that's why you have visitors who insisted on meeting with you first thing this morning. You haven't left home yet, have you?"

"No."

"Then hang up and get going. Connie Forsythe and her niece Emily Lombard are on their way. If you can get here before they do, I can explain why they asked for a meeting with you."

"I'm heading for the door. The reason I called you is that I've got a visit planned for us with two more of the 'other women' in the maestro's life. These are women from his more distant past—Maggie Knight and Margaret Landry. You need to arrange to have lunch with me today—here at my house. In fact, it's best if you arrange the afternoon off for both of us."

"Wow! Consider it done. This is going to be a very interesting day, isn't it?"

"I hope so," I replied. *In a way that helps us catch a killer before someone else ends up like Dave or Charlie*, I added silently.

18 AN UNHAPPY CHORUS

When I arrived at my office, Carol had coffee ready. I followed her into a small conference room behind the reception area. I'd brought a box of those cookies from home and she set out a few for our guests, who were due to arrive any minute. When she caught the scent of those cookies, the smile already on her face broadened.

"Ooh, cookies! *Purrfect* treats for your Cat Factory pals. You're a super *pawsome* boss!"

Uh-oh, cat puns. Carol had obviously had a cup of the coffee she'd poured for me when I arrived. It was more than that, though. Rapid fire cat puns were a dead giveaway that Carol was wound up. She was buzzing even more after popping one of those sugary cookies into her mouth.

"Meow! Those will *pawsitively cat*-a*pult* the conversation into high gear while they tell their *tail* of *furtive* encounters with that *tomcat* Dave Rollins." My mouth fell open and I stood there for a few seconds.

"I have no words. That's a lot of cat puns in one sentence even for you. What is going on?"

"I'm not playing a game of cat and mouse with you, boss. These two let the cat out of the bag…" I interrupted her before she could say more as I caught sight of Connie and Emily walking into the reception area. Connie waved, although the expression on her face was not a happy one. Carol turned and dashed out to greet them. I followed and the two of us escorted them into the conference room.

Once we settled in around the little table, Connie introduced us to her niece Emily. The lovely blonde with big blues eyes and an angelic face began to tear up immediately. Then tears slid down her cheek.

She'd make a great Arielle, I thought as the part of my brain saturated from decades of working for The Cat took over. In fact, she could play the role of any of the Marvelous Marley World shepherdesses, although I don't believe Max Marley had a new feature film starring his beloved princess-like characters in the works any time soon.

As I watched her, she opened a small clutch purse she carried. At first, I figured she was pulling a tissue from it to sop up those tears. She didn't stop, though, when Carol and Connie each offered her one. Snatching the tissues with one hand, the other dug around in her bag. When Emily pulled her hand out she clutched a diamond studded treble clef pin.

"Emily wants to explain. Don't you Emily? We thought since you and the detective who's been trying to reach Emily are close, you could help tell us the best way to approach him about this." Emily nodded in agreement with her aunt but didn't utter a word.

Her pale skin was all splotchy.

"Did Dave Rollins give that to you?" I asked speaking softly.

"Yes," she whispered in reply. Then in a louder voice she added, "The night someone killed him. I was there. I took it, but I didn't kill him. I chickened out on our date and ran away—like Cinderella fleeing the ball."

Carol looked sideways at me, not convinced. I wasn't entirely convinced, either. At least not that she imagined that evening to have been a prince and Cinderella encounter. Her aunt rolled her eyes, so I could tell she didn't buy it.

"Oh, stop with the fairytale nonsense and just tell the story as it actually happened. Cut the drama, too." Emily screwed up her face, not like she was going to cry more, but in anger. The splotches on her face turned a deeper red.

"Back off Aunt Connie. Dave invited me over for a private celebration. I knew what he meant by that. He was no prince, but I liked the guy and it was kind of exciting, so I agreed." She paused and sipped her coffee, looking less like a princess herself now.

"Did you leave the reception together?"

"Not exactly. Dave called a limo for me and went on home while I waited for the driver to pick me up. When I got to his house Dave let the limo in through the gate and met me at the front door. He gave the driver this huge tip—a hundred-dollar bill—and sent him away. The minute the door closed behind me, I started to feel uneasy like I'd made a mistake. Dave gave me a glass of champagne and this gorgeous red rose, but he must have been drinking at the gala because he was already tipsy. I started to worry that an old guy like him shouldn't get any drunker than he was already. What if he fell down or something?" Connie cleared her throat. I took it she wasn't any happier with Emily's emerging Florence Nightingale routine than she been about the Cinderella bit.

"What? He looked old and sick. What if more alcohol and er, um, romance wasn't good for him? Anyway, after he showed me around a little I told him I wasn't feeling well. He insisted that I go upstairs and see the view from the veranda before I left. It only took me thirty seconds after we walked through his office to the veranda to realize it adjoined his bedroom. When we were in his office, he showed me this." She pointed to the pin.

"When I saw it, I decided I had to get out of there. There must have been half a dozen women at the gala wearing the same pin. I wondered about it. I should have asked Aunt Connie where she got it. She and her women friends may not mind being one of the maestro's romance of the month club members, but not me." Connie shifted uncomfortably in her seat, shook her head and then rolled her eyes again. In response Emily stuck her tongue out at her aunt like a spoiled child. My image of her as Arielle was gone for good now! The budding family feud was growing old fast. It was time to move the story along.

"Okay, so what did you do then?"

"I told Dave I was sorry, but I had a splitting headache and had to go home."

"And?"

"Dave called the limo driver back. He gave me that pin and told me to go home. I felt sorry for him since he looked so sad, but I had to get out of there. I took the pin, gave him a hug, and then I ran down the stairs and out the front door. The limo driver must have been close because he was back inside the gate in, uh, like two minutes."

Hmm, I wondered, making a note to ask Jack if anyone had checked with the limo service about a driver being at Dave's house that night. Carol could do that or could at least find out which service we'd used that night to ferry VIP guests to and from the gala. Emily was silent but had started to weep again.

"What is it?" I asked. "Did something else happen?"

"No, not really. I can't be sure I shut the front door when I left. I read in one of the news reports that the door was found unlatched. Did I do that? Is it my fault someone got in and killed him?"

"No, I don't believe you should be worried about that." I didn't say anything further. Jack wouldn't approve of my giving her any information she didn't already have about how Dave Rollins died or where they found his body. If she hadn't shut the door securely when she left, it could explain how the vandal gained entry to destroy Dave's house, especially if Dave had left the back gate open. It wasn't her fault he'd been killed, though, given that his murder had taken place out on the cliff trail.

"That's a huge relief. Later, when I heard Dave was dead, I wished I'd asked the security guard to check the door. He probably did that on his own anyway, right?" Alarm bells went off in my head. I tried to play it cool.

"Security guard?"

"Yes. A big guy wearing a baseball cap and carrying a huge flashlight. He had on a dark-colored uniform with a security guard sign on it."

"Do you remember the company name on it?"

"No, not really. It was a black and gold and said security guard."

"How big was he? Big as in tall or hefty?"

"Both. Over six feet tall, I'm sure, and beefy like a bouncer at a club."

"Do you remember his hair or eye color or anything distinctive about his appearance?" Emily pondered my question before answering. I tried to recall what else Jack had asked Charlie Daniels when he tried to get him to describe the wolfman.

"The porchlight wasn't very bright. His hair and eyes were dark. No wait, that's not completely true. His head was covered with a hoodie attached to something he wore under that jacket. The hair poking out was a very light color. He scared me when he appeared out of nowhere, pointing that light at me. The light was so bright I had to shield my eyes. When he stepped closer to ask who I was and what I was doing there, he raised his arm. His sleeve pulled back and I saw a tattoo for a second when the limo pulled in and the headlights hit him."

"What sort of tattoo?"

"A letter, like an initial. More than one, maybe. Anyway, the guard took off as soon as the limo pulled up—even before I could answer his questions."

"Do you remember what letter you saw?"

"I'm not sure. It was drawn in an old-fashioned fancy way that made it hard to read. An "M" or "N" maybe. To be honest, it might not even be a letter from the alphabet. Is it important?"

"It could be. Do your best to remember what you can when you tell your story to the police. Why didn't you call and tell them you were at Dave's house that night?"

"I was embarrassed about the way I behaved— going there in the first place and then running off the way I did. When I heard he was dead under suspicious circumstances, I was scared. Dave was still alive when I left, but what if the police thought we fought it out that night and I killed him? Or they figured I vandalized his home or let someone in who did it? Maybe they'd blame me for leaving Dave's door open on purpose, so someone could get in and kill him? It wouldn't be great for my reputation if it gets out that I was the mystery woman at his home for a romantic interlude or whatever they're calling it in the media coverage." Emily unleashed that litany of excuses at breakneck speed. If she had more to say, Connie put an end to it.

"That's enough!" Connie commanded, in such a loud voice I was startled. She was clearly more than a little miffed at her niece. "If they find out you were at the house that night, so what? You decided to go there for a romantic interlude, Cinderella. You decided to leave, taking that little diamond pin with you. At least you're alive to feel embarrassed or scared or concerned about what will happen if the news gets out that you were with that old man, as you've called him, on the night he was murdered. Dave Rollins had his problems, but he didn't deserve to die like that and you were one of the last people to see him alive!" Connie teared up at that point.

"Some of us members of the romance of the month club loved him even if he didn't deserve it. Dave was chasing a dream—a romantic fantasy rather than a real woman. It hurt to be consigned to the unhappy chorus of women in the maestro's life. Love's hard to find and harder to hang onto, isn't it?"

Connie looked at me and then at Carol as if wondering if we understood. I nodded. After my first love died, I gave up on the idea I'd ever find love again. Unlike Dave Rollins, however, I didn't even try. Then Jack Wheeler waltzed into my life and everything changed. I felt a sudden wave of sadness for Dave and all the women who'd cared about him as deeply as Connie.

"I'm sorry, Aunt Connie." Emily reached out and put an arm around her aunt's shoulders. Then she pulled her arm back, squared her shoulders, and faced me. "Tell me what I have to do to get this mess cleared up."

"You need to speak to the police and get your story on record. I'm sure they'll want it in writing, too, and will ask you for a signed statement. I'll call Detective Wheeler and he'll have someone contact you to set a time for you to meet with them. If you saw that guard again, would you recognize him?" Emily's face began to flush again with fear or anger, or both. She scanned the room, eying the door as if she might bolt!

"How do I know? Maybe! What if he recognizes me? I want my lawyer, before I agree to do anything. In fact, I'm out of here until I have a talk with him!"

"Don't even think about it," her aunt said. Connie reached out and placed a hand on her niece's arm. "If you want to get this over, calm down, and do as Georgie says. You'll have to tell your story one more time and then it'll be done. She can have her lawyer with her, right?"

"She's a witness not a suspect, but I'm sure she can have legal representation with her." I glanced at Emily wondering if she was telling us the whole truth about what went on that night. Figuring that out would have to be up to the police investigators. As far as I could tell, we were done here. "You've done the right thing, you two. Your Aunt Connie's got your best interests at heart and she's right, this is your best chance to bring the matter to a close." In another couple of minutes, the two women were gone again.

"I was right about this being an interesting day, wasn't I?" Carol asked.

"Yes, and there's more to come. Are you ready for round two with Margaret Landry and Margaret Knight—or Meg and Maggie as they prefer to be called."

"I can't wait to meet them and hear their stories about the maestro."

"I'll be surprised if Maggie has much to tell. She was remarkably upbeat on the phone, given how hard this must be on her. To lose her grandfather so soon after entering his life has to be tough."

"It can't be easy for her grandmother either. Maybe Maggie's putting up a good front for Meg."

"Let's go over the plans we have for the memorial service. That way we'll be able to give them a good sense about what we have in mind to honor his professional accomplishments once he came to work for Marvelous Marley World. To be honest, what I'm most curious about is what his life was like before that even though it's not particularly relevant to the memorial we're planning."

"Meg Landry ought to be able to tell you plenty about it."

"If she's willing and I can figure out how to steer the conversation that way. I'd like to ask her the sort of questions the police are most likely to ask about anyone from his past who might still want to kill him. It doesn't feel good to add to the distress they're feeling."

"If they believe it'll help figure out who killed Dave, they'll be more than willing to answer your questions. I'll be surprised if Maggie Knight turns out to be a spoiled brat like Emily Lombard. That chick got on my nerves. She needs to take a few lessons from her Aunt Connie who still has a heart even after one of those bad break-ups with the maestro."

"Pat mentioned Connie wasn't always as dispassionate as she is now about Dave's shortcomings. Emily's young, maybe she'll improve with age. Let's see if the other women in Dave's life are easier to take and if they have any information that can help. Emily Lombard wasn't in the maestro's life long enough to know much about him or care. At least one of the Margarets we're about to meet was in Dave's life a long time—even before he was Dave."

19 THE TWO MARGARETS

Carol set the table outside, prepared the baby vegetables and tiny potatoes I planned to serve with the Sole Meunière. She played with the cats while I cooked the lunch items that could be prepared in advance and prepped items that needed to be cooked on the spot. As often as I've cooked meals for others, I still get anxious. At least until the cooking starts. Once that happens, the wonderful colors, textures, and aromas involved in cooking take over. It's a more sensual than cerebral experience that sends worries fleeing. I'm fortunate not to have developed more of an addiction to food than to coffee and chocolate.

Before the doorbell rang, Miles' trumpet blast of a voice announced their arrival. Carol and I dashed to the door to greet them. I could tell instantly that the two women were related. Margaret Landry was the taller of the two, even while leaning a bit on a cane. It was easy to believe Teddy Austin's tale of what a gorgeous woman she was when he met her in Chicago as Dave's "Aunt Meg."

She was still stunning with her hair pulled back in a French twist adorned with a cloisonné comb. It was still shiny even though it was no longer black. Her eyes were as startling as Teddy had said.

"Come in, Maggie, please. I'm so glad you could join me for lunch at the last minute like this. It's a pleasure to meet you," I said extending a hand to Margaret Landry. "I'm Georgie Shaw and this is my Executive Assistant, Carol Ripley."

"Believe it or not…" Carol interjected nervously. "I used to get teased a lot as a kid because of my last name." The two Margarets looked as though they weren't sure what to say. I smiled and gave Carol a nudge.

"That's one of Carol's favorite ways to introduce herself. She's hard to forget later, trust me." The women smiled.

"A built-in mnemonic, huh? Clever. I'm glad to meet you, too. Please call me Meg. Thanks for inviting us to lunch, Georgie," she said shaking hands with me and then with Carol. Meg's eyes swept the room as we moved from the foyer into the open great room and kitchen area. "Is there no end to magnificent homes with ocean views in Southern California?" She asked as she kept moving, drawn toward the sliders that led out to the veranda overlooking the Pacific Ocean.

In our exchange of greetings, I'd completely ignored the cats. Miles was having none of that! He leaped to a barstool, leaned back his head, and roared. Ella jumped up next to him, blinking her beautiful blue eyes at our guests.

"I forgot to introduce you to the lord of the

manor and his lady fair. Meet Miles—as in Miles Davis, and the lovely Ella," I said as the two women gave the furry duo the attention they demanded.

"As in Ella Fitzgerald?" I nodded in response to Meg's question as the princess earned her moniker by uttering a series of sweet melodious gurgles followed by another trumpet blast from Miles. "That was impressive, Miles. The maestro liked to say, 'If you've got something to say, say it loud enough to be heard in the back of the room.' A lesson he learned early playing in noisy bars and clubs in New Orleans and surrounding bayou towns." She pronounced it "N'awlins" exaggerating the cadence as she dragged out the one word that counted as two.

"How is it that Dave Rollins had almost no accent? Yours is subtle, too. Even your voice, Maggie, doesn't give you away as a woman born and raised in Southern Louisiana," I commented.

"Dave and I both had elocution lessons as children. Our families were dead set against sounding like locals. Not as any aspiration to be 'Yankees,' mind you. Their affections lay with their French ancestry and a desire to convey a certain *je ne sais quoi* that they imagined to be Continental. Dave and I spoke French right along with English we learned from bilingual nannies. In Maggie's case, it's all about not getting typecast when she auditions for roles." Carol opened the sliders and led us out to our table set for al fresco dining on the veranda. The breeze that floated up to us captured a lovely scent.

"That's a wonderful fragrance!" I said.

"More Francophilia, I'm afraid. An old French fragrance my mother adored, and I adopted. Dave loved it, too, and bought it for me. After so many years, it has become an old friend—a source of solace and comfort."

We seated ourselves and began eating the crusty warm bread and creamy white bean soup I'd prepared as an appetizer. Meg's mention of solace had been laden with a note of sadness. Perhaps because neither her mother nor Dave were alive to enjoy the fragrance she wore. The pounding of the ocean filled the pause in our conversation.

"This is delicious," Maggie said breaking into the silence.

"Yes, it's perfect. The setting and the view, too. I'm so overcome by it, I can hardly speak!"

"Our soup is only the beginning."

"Carol's right. In fact, I need to head back inside and prepare our next course. Please, enjoy your soup and the view while I finish the dish."

"May I come inside and keep you company while Carol and Maggie chat? Maggie is curious about what it's like to work for The Cat. She was relentless in questions put to her grandfather about The Cat Factory. I have a few questions for you about other matters." Meg gave me no hint of what those questions might be, but I was more than a little interested in hearing them.

"Follow me, Meg. You're in luck, Maggie. There's no one better to ask about Marvelous Marley World than Carol. She's an expert on more than what goes on in the Food and Beverage Division where we work." It was as if a fuse had been lit. Maggie sat up straight and shifted her seat a little toward Carol.

"That would be great! Grandpa was so fixated on

his music that I could not get him to help me understand how what he did fit into the rest of what goes on at Marvelous Marley World."

"Marvelous Marley World is to Carol as France was to your parents, Meg. Right?" Carol nodded in response to my question with great enthusiasm.

"I'll admit it. I love The Cat Factory—call it Cat-factoryphilia! Where should I begin? Do you want an overview of how it all works today, or do you want to hear the spiel about how Max and his friends like your grandfather started out?"

"At the beginning—at least at the point where my grandfather joined Max. Grandpa loved that 'crazy old mad man' as he called Max so often."

"They're going to be at it for a while. Let's go cook!" I stepped into the kitchen with Meg close behind.

"May I help or is it better to stay out of the way?"

"I've done as much as I could in advance," I said as I walked around the large, granite-topped kitchen island. "You can help me in a few minutes. For now, please try the wine we're having for lunch and make yourself comfortable."

My kitchen island has "step downs" so that part of it is at standing height with plenty of work space. Opposite is a higher elevation with tall barstools for guests. Then it drops down to seating level. Both sets of seats provide a good view of what I'm doing in the kitchen and allow me to speak to guests while I cook. Meg sat down in one of the comfy chairs at the seating level where Jack and I often have breakfast on workdays.

"My mise en place, see?" I said as I pulled a tray from the refrigerator laden with the items for our main course.

"Yes—'setting in place' all the elements for a dish is handy. Maggie googled you and found out about your chef training. I can tell it's useful to you at home as well as at work."

"Home is about the only chance I have to do much cooking these days. On occasion, I pitch in when we're opening a new kitchen or revamping the menu, but mostly I manage the food and beverages others prepare. How is the wine?" I asked as I poured clear butter into a large sauté pan.

"Fresh and lively—delicious. Ah! Clarified butter and sole fillets! Sole Meunière—you have gone out of your way for me! I will never be able to thank you for your thoughtfulness."

"I enjoy this dish, too. As did, Dave." I hoped that might steer the conversation back to the topic of Dave and his past life. I was dying with curiosity about the questions she had for me. "Dave and I weren't close, but we worked together for a long time and I learned a few things about him. He earned every bit of the recognition he received. I'm not sure how he found the time to do all he did."

"Given all the time he spent chasing women, you mean?" I carefully placed the dredged sole fillets into the sauté pan and then stopped for a moment to gauge Meg's take on the remark she'd made. She wore a wistful, almost melancholy expression. "I blame myself, given what a devastating toll our love affair took on him. His family disowned him. Most of his snobby friends did, too. Even though I came from the same society circles, I became a persona non grata when I married Robert Landry. Adultery didn't make me more unwelcome than I already was in those circles. By falling in love with me, Dan Devereaux, which was his name then, was shunned, too."

"Dave must have learned something from that experience because I never detected a hint of snobbery from him. He did a good deal over the years to make the Music Group at Marvelous Marley World more diverse. Dave was always welcoming to everyone he encountered regardless of their background as far as I could tell."

"Oh, yes. I've seen plenty over the years about how welcoming he was to a bevy of beauties once he became a celebrity. The haunted look in his eyes made me feel horribly guilty. I loved him, but I didn't have the courage to stand up to my husband." Meg stopped to sip her wine before going on with her story.

"Dan left town and changed his name because the ruthless psychopath I'd married threatened to kill him. Beating him to a pulp wasn't enough. Not just because of our affair, but because that horrid husband of mine embroiled Dave in his dirty business. The police arrested Dave, and Robert threatened to have him killed while he was locked up. The wretched man had that kind of clout at the time, so I presume he could have made good on the threat. Dave decided his only option was to get out. He wanted to take me with him, but I sent him away by himself. If I'd left with him, Robert would have put out a bounty on my head and every lowlife in Southern Louisiana would have been searching for us. I couldn't stay away from Dave, and probably put us both at risk by visiting him in Chicago. When I discovered I was pregnant, I knew I had to end that for us and our baby. The irony is, once I became a mother, Robert lost interest in me as a woman and spent most of his time in a lavish suite at one of the hotels he owned. At least he left me alone, although he would never have agreed to a divorce. After Deirdre was born, there weren't any more children."

"Did Dave ever try to contact you? Was he aware that you had a child?"

"Every year on my birthday I received a single red rose and a musical charm with a note signed with the letter 'D' inside a heart." She laughed before going on. "I'm so old now that there are too many to wear on a bracelet. I keep them in a velvet display case I had made especially for them. While my daughter was alive, I kept them hidden. When she was young, I was afraid of the questions she might ask about them. As she grew older, she rebelled, sought out Robert's company, and fell under his spell. I feared she'd steal them or tell him about them and that would cause trouble for Dave. Maybe if I'd told her about Dave and insisted she spend time with him, her life would have gone in a different direction."

I was the one who was spellbound. I turned over the fillets, and then placed a second pan on the stove to sauté the parboiled fresh baby vegetables that would accompany our sole. I also peeked at the potatoes I'd put into the oven when our guests had arrived.

"Ah, that's what I smelled when we came into the kitchen a few minutes ago."

"Roasted baby potatoes with Herbs de

Provence," I said, satisfied that all the components of our meal were about to finish together. "Only a few more minutes."

"I'm not sure how much you know about Deirdre, but her life was devastating, most of all to herself, but it was hard on Maggie and me, too."

"Only a little. What I learned came from Dave's attorney when Jack and I discussed Dave's estate. To our surprise, that included provisions he'd made for a granddaughter. Deirdre Knight came up during our conversation. From what he said, I can only guess at how difficult it must have been for you."

"Our own private little Shakespearean tragedy. She died nearly two decades ago and it's still hard to understand how it all went so wrong. Did Dave's attorney tell you how to find me?"

"No. Dave's attorney and his accountant are both under the impression that you're no longer alive." Meg laughed. This time her laugh was a hearty one. Almost musical, it sounded so much like Maggie's.

"Dave has done so much for Maggie and me— once she revealed herself to him. She wants a career in show business, so Maggie's committed to staying on the West Coast. Dave didn't want her to be alone and sent for me. I have this dreadful worry, though, that it's what got him killed. Is that possible?"

"There's no reason to believe that at this point. It's too soon, I'm afraid, to say who killed him. Jack and his colleagues have lots of evidence to sift through. They've conducted dozens of interviews already and will get around to you and Maggie soon now that they know you exist. It's possible Dave was killed because of some connection to his past. Robert Landry's been dead a long time, now. From what you've said, you and your husband had gone your separate ways even before that."

"That's what I keep telling myself. I'd hate to think that after forgoing the chance to have a lifetime together, Maggie and I stirred up old trouble for Dave and he ended up dead anyway."

"Does Robert Landry have family who would want to seek revenge because of Daniel Devereaux's affair with you or his involvement in the family business?"

"No. Robert Landry was the black sheep of a moldy old southern family with little to their name other than a rundown plantation that was largely swamp. If I'd turned up dead at the foot of the Malibu cliffs, you might want to see if any members of the Devereaux family had visited California recently. I can't think of one of them who cared enough about Dave to go to that much trouble. Not me either, if I'm honest. I can hear it now, 'Meg Landry isn't worth the powder it would take to blow her up.' No, I don't how anyone from the Devereaux family who could have been responsible for killing Dave any more than the Landrys."

"Given the way in which you've described Robert Landry, it sounds like there was no love lost between him and the people with whom he did business."

"That's an understatement. One or more of his so-called partners set him up."

"The statute of limitations must have long ago run out on any wrongdoing Dave learned about while he was mixed up in Robert's dirty business. Would anyone among Robert's business associates care enough to avenge him or have some reason to worry about something Dave learned so long ago?"

"I don't know, but I was oblivious to Robert's business. On purpose since I turned a blind eye to it—see no evil, hear no evil, and no one can lean on you to speak about the evil. That was Robert's philosophy on the matter and I went along with it to keep the peace. There was a threat behind that philosophy too. Now I can see it as another failure to stand up to the man."

"He was a dangerous man to oppose. Once you had Deirdre to consider, what could you have done?"

"I wish I'd tried. Despite my efforts to protect her, she ended up dead too soon thanks, in large part, to Robert Landry. He let her run wild with Harry Knight and his crowd."

"Children make their own choices. It's obvious to me, she pursued a relationship with him, against your wishes and all the motherly advice you gave her."

"That's for sure. Dave's brother, Bill, might be able to tell you more about Robert's business associates. He didn't wise up and escape as quickly as Dave did. When Deirdre was accused of killing her husband, Bill was still around. He tried to help her, so he can tell you more about the web of people with whom she'd become entangled. I don't know why anyone in Deirdre's circle would have it in for Dave. Bill maybe, but not Dave."

"The name we have for him is Bill Rollins like Dave, not Devereaux." Meg nodded.

"I know. Eventually William Devereaux did the same thing Daniel had done. After Robert was killed, Bill left without telling me where he was going or why. Dave told me recently that he'd changed his name to William Rollins at some point. I spoke to Bill briefly when he called Dave a couple of weeks ago. It didn't seem appropriate to go into the past over the phone, but I do know how to reach him."

"Carol called and left a voicemail message inviting him to the memorial service and asked him to call me. We'll see if that happens."

"I'll make sure he responds to your call. I don't know what the rules are about receiving or returning calls—family can always reach him." I was puzzled, wondering if that meant Bill's involvement in Robert's dirty business had caught up with him and he was in prison somewhere.

"As Bill Rollins, he became a teacher at St. Mary's School for Boys until he retired. The school is on the grounds of a religious community that's not exactly cloistered, but Bill's still living there. They have rules about how 'Brother Bill' communicates with the outside world."

"That puts a new twist on things, doesn't it?"

"It does. Here's a question I hope you can answer for me. Who can Maggie trust? Dave is gone. I won't be around forever. What about his attorney and the accountant? Maggie said she liked them both. Why would Dave have told them I was dead?"

"Hmm, that is a good question, isn't it? Are you sure he told them you were dead, or did they just assume it since he made no mention of your whereabouts when Maggie showed up?" My recollection was that Skip had said it in a very matter of fact way.

"I'm not certain how they arrived at that conclusion. Maggie heard them say it when Dave took her to meet them. It wasn't too long after she moved out here. She mentioned it to me because Dave hadn't made any effort to correct them. Maggie took her cue from him and didn't say anything either. When she asked him about it later, Dave responded in a frustratingly enigmatic way."

"How so?"

"He said, 'People aren't always as they seem.' If that's the case, why would he do business with them?"

I flashed for a moment on Jennifer's odd demeanor during the meeting we'd had with her and my suspicion that she and Dave might have been more than friends at some point. Not only that, but the fact that Jack had caught her watching us as we returned to our car had screamed "up to no good" to me. I hadn't asked Jack about it again. I would now after pondering Meg's astute questions.

"Dave has relied on them for years to manage his finances, his estate, and other legal matters. The firm also has ties to Marvelous Marley World and our CEO with whom Dave was very close. Maybe it was too sensitive an issue to raise, or too difficult to cut them loose as complicated as his estate has become." I was still mulling over her question when she asked a new one.

"What about Pat Dolan?"

"Well she knows you're alive if that's any indication of Dave's belief about her trustworthiness.

He also entrusted her to handle the arrangements involved in relocating you and Maggie to California."

"She's always been kind to Maggie and me. Helpful, too." Meg's voice trailed off as she reached the end of her remarks.

"Did Dave say something about her that has you worried?" I asked.

"Not directly, but he came to visit one afternoon, and he was preoccupied. When I asked him why, he said he'd been searching for something and couldn't find it. I tried to reassure him that people our age often misplaced items and he didn't need to be concerned. That's when he said he wasn't worried about his memory but feared that someone he trusted had taken it. When I pressed him about it, he changed the subject, like he'd done with Maggie after that comment about people not being what they seem. Now that someone has killed him, I wish Maggie and I had taken his concerns more seriously."

"Did he say what it was that had gone missing?"

"I wasn't sure what he was talking about, but I believe he said he was searching for a medallion of some kind."

"He must have been referring to one of the gold medallions Max awarded him over the years. It was Max's way of honoring the maestro's success for setting a new sales record, getting nominated, or winning an award. When there was a new one, we always saw it first. Dave kept them on display in his home office." It was my turn for my voice to trail off. Had the thief murdered Dave and staged a burglary to cover up the missing medallions? Why not smash the glass on the display case and take more of them, or steal other items in Dave's house to make it look like the intrusion was about theft if the whole scheme was intended to be a cover up?

"I can understand your misgivings, Meg. Why not have Maggie find someone new to trust until the investigation into Dave's murder gets resolved and his estate it settled."

"You?"

"I'm happy to do what I can, of course. She needs a good lawyer to head off any hanky-panky about Dave's last will and testament. Let me get her the name of a good attorney who's not associated with Marvelous Marley World or any of the parties already in Dave's life."

"If you could do that, I'd rest more easily. After all we've been through, I don't want more trouble for her."

"I'm with you on that one hundred percent. I'll get a couple of names for her, she can meet them both, and decide which one's a better fit. Let's eat!"

I plated the food, placed the plates on a serving tray, and had Margaret open the screen door for me as we headed back outside for our lunch. Thankfully, the meal turned out well enough, despite being so engrossed in Meg's revelations. We chatted amiably over lunch about Maggie and Meg's adjustment to life on the West Coast. A thoroughly enjoyable conversation that was suddenly interrupted by a phone call. Not mine, to my great relief.

"Will you excuse me for a moment? I need to take this call." Maggie picked up her purse hanging on the back of her chair and dug through it as she stepped through the sliding doors into the kitchen.

Whether she knew it or not, from where I sat I could see two cats stalking her.

A few minutes later, Maggie came dashing back outside. With her phone still in hand, she dropped back into her chair next to me. She wore a huge smile on her face.

"I got the part! Can you believe that? It's a bit part as the goofy girl next door to the star, but it's a recurring role in a new sitcom. If the show gets off the ground, I'll be working as an actress for a while."

"Congratulations!" Carol and I exclaimed almost in unison.

"That's wonderful!" Meg exclaimed. "There are no small parts, as I'm sure you've heard many times."

"Grandpa said the same thing." For a moment, Maggie's mood darkened. I felt her sadness about not being able to share the news with Dave. Then it was as if a spotlight had been turned on her. She lit up. "He's still looking out for me, isn't he? I haven't even told you the best thing about the role is that the goofy neighbor is a wannabe singer, like me. I'll get to sing as well as act."

"A role made in heaven," I murmured wondering if Dave's old friend Max might also have had a hand in helping her get consideration for the role. I heard a soft thud from inside, followed by other odd sounds.

"Maggie, you're going to need someone to review the contract for that job before you sign it," I said making eye contact with Meg for a second. "Why don't I send you the name of a couple of lawyers who can help you with that and anything that comes up having to do with your grandfather's estate, okay?"

"A lawyer! I am moving up in the world. Thanks,

Georgie." Maggie's response drew an appreciative nod from her grandmother. Another strange sound from indoors shifted my attention.

"Those cats are up to something, I bet! I'll go check on them. I hope you saved room for dessert because Maggie's news calls for a celebration. I've got mascarpone brownies with a little vanilla ice cream, okay? Coffee, too—the real deal or decaf—whichever you prefer."

"I'm on a roll. Chocolate brownies, too!" Maggie replied enthusiastically. Meg laughed at Maggie's enthusiastic response. "Decaf for me please, I'm already wired."

"Who can live without chocolate and coffee? I'll have decaf too since I know Maggie will worry less about me if I skip the caffeine, even after I got such a good report card from the doctor this morning." This was a woman after my own heart! Both Margarets were great fun to have around. Jack would enjoy meeting them. I was already formulating plans for a dinner party.

"Do you want help?" Carol offered. I was about to say no when I saw Ella go scurrying by at lightning speed. Miles, on her heels, bellowed as he gave chase.

"Maybe you'd better come along, Carol, in case the cats knock me down as they rampage." As if to underscore my concern, Ella scurried by going the other way. I caught sight of something shiny she was batting around like a hockey puck.

"What is that you, furry little devil?" I hurried into the house with Carol following. My response was the pleasurable chatter that means Ella has acquired a new beloved object. Ella kept moving but Miles came to a stop, eyed me, kinked his tale and took off in pursuit of Ella who was heading down the hallway with her toy. "Uh-oh," I said as I spotted Maggie's soft leather purse on the ground, some of its contents on the floor.

"Carol, will you put Maggie's stuff back into her purse, please? Let me go see what the little sneak thief has stolen." Ella's not above cat burgling if that's what it takes to feed her need for shiny things. As Carol went to work stuffing items back into Maggie's purse, I took off after the cats.

This time they both stopped and looked right at me. Then, zoom, they were off again. The only thing that slowed them down was the fact that she couldn't move too fast with her loot. When I caught up with them, I understood Ella's delight. I picked up what was an exquisite silver compact etched with a fanciful and elaborate letter "M." I stared at the beautifully drawn letter, marveling at the handiwork, and couldn't help thinking that "M" stood for murder as often as it had popped up in the past few days.

"Oh, Ella, this is so pretty, isn't it?" She blinked at me. Leaning against me, she stood on her hind legs and reached up for it. "Shame on you, Ella, for stealing from our guests. That's rude!" Then Ella griped at me, dropped down on all fours, and showed me her backside. As she shuffled on down the hall to sulk in the bedroom, Miles trotted after her without uttering a sound. No back talk told me he knew Ella was at fault.

Talk about an inside job, I thought as I took that lovely compact back to its rightful owner. Was someone close to Dave also a compulsive sneak thief like Ella, or worse—willing to kill to possess those shiny gold medallions? Jack was going to love hearing the bits and pieces of news from all the other women Carol and I had spoken to today. I couldn't wait!

20 REQUIESCAT IN PACE

I was glad to be sitting down when I called Jack to tell him about what I'd learned from my meeting with Emily Lombard and lunch with Meg and Maggie. He was relieved to hear I was already at home, behind guard gates, and a home security system. Before we were married, Jack had insisted I improve my home security system. An all too close encounter with a Marvelous Marley World associate who turned up at my house one night had been a scary reminder that gated communities don't always keep the bad guys out. I was glad I'd listened to Jack after his latest update about Charlie's murder.

"Charlie's killer left a calling card with a note on it. Scrawled on the back is the Latin phrase: 'requiescat in pace' or something close to that as far as my pronunciation goes. It means rest in peace. I'm sure that must be what the wolfman said about the photograph of Dave Rollins when he gave it to Charlie."

"It's hard to imagine how Charlie got 'request it in pieces' from that, but I'm sure you're right."

"Well, there's more to it than Charlie's translation. The phrase turns up on shreds in that composite I asked for of the torn note paper found around the stairs. You were right about the song you identified from the first scrap of paper. Along with more of the musical notation, that Latin phrase for rest in peace is written on it, too, in bold, florid calligraphy."

"You must be kidding, Jack!"

"I wish I were. I'm afraid there's more."

"Okay," I muttered, brought up short by the ominous tone in my husband's voice.

"When I told you Charlie's killer left a calling card, I should have been more specific. I wanted to make sure you were safe first. The killer scrawled that Latin phrase on the back of one of your business cards, Georgie." That's the point at which I felt a shot of adrenalin that made me feel weak in the knees, and grateful to be seated. I was speechless trying to understand the implications—none of which seem harmless or purely coincidental.

"Are you still there?"

"Yes, I'm here. Just about anyone can get one of my business cards easily enough. I hand them out all over town. Most recently at Dave's gala. They don't have to get one directly from me either. We leave them out at information desks at all the resort hotels, in restaurants, and on the counter in the reception area at Marvelous Marley World Headquarters. The caterers carry them…" Jack interrupted me.

"You'll drive yourself nuts trying to figure out

how it got into the hands of Charlie's killer. What matters is for you to pay extra attention to your personal safety, especially when you and Carol are nosing into anything remotely related to Dave's life or death. Cool it, even."

"You're not going to lock me in a closet or our bedroom, are you?" I asked hoping to lighten up my mood and the tone of our conversation.

"What?"

"Oh, it's something Carol said about how we're like Nick and Nora Charles—from *The Thin Man* movies, you know?"

"Yes, I do. You're not an heiress but I did luck out like Nick, didn't I?"

"Your luck will run out quick if you ever pull a stunt like Nick did trying to get Nora to butt out of a case. That and his devotion to the life of the vine are drawbacks to an otherwise charming man in an entertaining series."

"My only vice, other than you, is your cooking. Especially the desserts. Those cookies went over big. Unfortunately, that started all the quips again about marrying up." Jack let out an exasperated sigh, and then spoke in a high, squeaky tone, 'And she bakes, too!'"

"Let me guess—Artie Dodge."

"Yep, or the 'artful dodger' as he's better known around here given how often he manages to avoid doing his share of paperwork. He was Johnny-on-the-spot when those cookies appeared."

"I'm glad your coworkers enjoyed them. As I recall, 'poor Nicky,' as Nora called him, took plenty of ribbing from his pals. At least, since I'm not an heiress, you don't have to put up with nasty remarks from snooty family members."

"That is so true. Your brothers have welcomed me with open arms, grateful I rescued their sister from a life as an old maid." I gasped.

"Shame on you! That comment's almost as bad as locking me in a closet. Besides, I won't be getting any older as a married woman if that killer on the loose decides to sneak up on me and bash me over the head. If you use that old maid lingo around my women friends, married or not, you may be the one who gets a bump on the head."

"I'm sorry to tease you about being an old maid. You're far too pretty for anyone to believe me anyway."

"And here comes the blarney. Enough about me. You've got to hear what Emily Lombard had to say including the fact that she was at Dave's house Friday night. With prodding from her Aunt Connie, Emily agreed to provide a written statement and sit down for an interview if her lawyer's present. She's expecting a phone call from you or someone with the Malibu police."

"That's great. We won't have to continue chasing her down."

It didn't take long to give Jack the scoop about Emily's version of what went on Friday night. I warned him that the sweet-looking, blue-eyed blonde was no angel. She might not be as cooperative with her lawyer in the room as she'd been with her Aunt Connie confronting her. As I knew it would, the part of her story about bumping into a security guard got Jack's attention.

"Accosted sounds more like it. She was lucky that limo showed up when it did. Once I've confirmed the time the limo picked up Emily, I'll check again with Dave's security service to see if anyone was patrolling the area around then. Unless Dave had called them, they wouldn't be making a patrol on foot anyway."

"I agree. He struck me as intimidating. It wasn't just his size, either. When she described him as big and beefy, Adam popped into my head. Does he qualify as beefy—as in bar bouncer beefy?"

"Mm, maybe. Bar bouncer beefy or not, he's a big guy with access to Dave's property. I didn't see any tattoos, did you?"

"No, dang it! Then again, I wasn't looking for them, were you?"

"No. Let's ask Pat, now that she's turned over a new leaf when it comes to sharing what she knows with us. If he's got a tattoo, we'll pick him up; and when Emily Lombard comes in for her interview, we'll see if she can I.D. him as the fake security guard."

"Wouldn't it be great if it were that simple? I'd love to make that kind of progress now that I know there's a card-carrying Georgie-hater out there."

"I agree, but it's been less than a week since Dave was killed. In homicide investigation years that's no time at all."

"I hope they're shorter than dog years. I don't like the idea of more bodies turning up, especially if one of them could be mine."

"Hope's a good thing, but keeping your guard up is even better. Hang on a second and let me get someone to follow up with Emily Lombard. I'm also going to get someone to see if Dave's security service had anyone on the premises or nearby that night. As far as I recall, they do drive-by checks but no foot patrols. Then, I want to hear what you learned from Maggie Knight and Margaret Landry. It could wait until I get home, but if you tell me before I leave for the day, I can get someone working on any leads they provided. Don't go anywhere."

"Don't worry. That's not going to happen." While I waited for Jack to return, I compulsively checked the locks on the doors and alarm system. All silly and needless actions. It was dark out and I kept picturing my business card in a dead man's shirt pocket with a note on it. Rest in peace, in any language conveys the same unpleasant message.

Something in my movements put the cats on guard. They were on my heels as I made my rounds and not making a sound. There had to be a connection between all the disparate components. Women and Mozart, art and money, were recurring themes at the center of this mess. How did they fit together and what did they have to do with me?

An image of Maggie's compact Ella had found so delightful came back to me. "Let's not forget the stupid letter 'M'!" I griped aloud. The sudden sound of my voice startled the cats and they took off. "Fraidy cats!" I exclaimed, speaking to myself too as I emerged from the paranoid reverie that had overcome me. When Jack came back on the phone a second later, I had a question for him.

"Did you or your coworkers have any luck finding out more about the members of the Wolf

Gang or any tie-in between that group and all the Mozart mumbo-jumbo that keeps turning up in the investigation?"

"Not much. Pratt and Kendall are dead, as Pat told us. We confirmed that Professor James Bellagio is still alive. He won't be back on campus until tomorrow after being out of the country for the past ten days or so. That makes it unlikely he killed Dave even if he did have an old score to settle with him. There's also the matter of his age. I hate to tarnish my knight in shining armor image, but I'd find it difficult to dump a bucket of rocks on anyone at my age. If our assailant and Dave's killer were one and the same, Professor Bellagio isn't likely to be our man."

"I'm still blinded by the sheen on your armor, Sir Jack! Do you have any reason to believe there was trouble among the members of the Wolf Gang?"

"No. I tracked down one of the two younger men in that photo who served the maestro and his gang members when they met back in the nineties. He still works for the City Club as a maître d'. Gil Evans remembered them and even told me which private dining room they were in when that photo was taken. He laughed when I asked if he'd ever witnessed any arguments that got out of hand. Gil Evans claims there was endless arguing, but no brawling or challenges to resolve their differences with a duel like Pat says Dave and Max did that day."

"What were the Wolf Gang members arguing about?" I asked.

"Mostly Mozart—his music and his life. That included the dispute about Salieri and his envy of Mozart that supposedly led him to commit murder."

"That mystery hasn't ever been resolved one way or the other. I went back and read about it again and it's not clear Salieri was all that envious of Mozart since he was a high-profile composer with a successful career in his own right. There's no clear evidence that Mozart was poisoned by Salieri, either, even though he believed that's what was happening to him as he grew sicker. What complicated matters is that Salieri confessed to poisoning Mozart when he was near death years later. His doctor claimed he'd descended into dementia by then."

"Maybe a last-ditch effort to make a name for himself as the man who killed Mozart."

"Good grief. All we need is another motive. Kill the maestro and achieve instant stardom!" I stomped my foot in frustration.

"Whether it's true or not, that character Skip mentioned who wrote Dave all those letters over the years believed the whole Salieri assassin story."

"Pat said they hadn't heard from him in several months. It is odd the letters he wrote to Dave are one of the few items Pat has identified as missing after the break-in. Maybe he was the intruder in Dave's house that night and he searched the place to find those letters."

"Or someone wants us to believe Dave's life has been turned upside down by the guy who wrote them. Something about this just seems too theatrical to me. A wolfman who mixes in pieces of sheet music with Latin phrases on it and who signed his letters with a florid initial 'M' seems like a cheesy script for a bad 'B' movie. I'd give it a title like '*M*' *as in Murder not Mozart*."

"Here's another odd incident involving the letter 'M.' Maggie had a compact with her today. Dave gave Margaret Landry that compact when he first fell in love with her. It's exquisitely etched with an ornate letter 'M.' That's 'M' as in Margaret, not Mozart or murder."

"Oh, good grief, that has to be a coincidence, doesn't it?"

"Curiouser and curiouser, huh?" I asked stealing a line from Lewis Carol.

"Yes, I'd say so. There are plenty of Alice in Wonderland moments in a murder investigation, but this one seems to have more than most. I can't even blame it on the Marvelous Marley World connection since there's not a cartoon character mixed up in this anywhere. Even Max has kept his nose out of it." As Jack uttered those last words, I was overcome by a wave of superstition in a "speak of the devil" way.

"Let's count our blessings. If my suspicions are correct, Max is busy pulling strings from behind the scenes. I'll bet you Max not only knows about Maggie but helped her get a break with her career today." I explained what I meant by sharing the news Maggie received during our lunch today.

"Good for him. He's better off doing that than trying to huff and puff his way into the investigation of Dave's murder."

"Hey, he's succeeded in doing that already which is why both of us are up to our necks in this mess. Let me tell you the rest of what went on at lunch. Meg Landry gave me a few more details about Dave's past as Daniel Devereaux." I gave Jack a quick overview of our discussion, surprised at how quick it went. Meg's story had such an impact on me at the time, but little of substance had come from it.

"I can draw a couple of conclusions from Meg's story. First, despite the fact Meg has this uneasy feeling she and Maggie triggered events that led to Dave's death, she came up empty. No motive. No person from his past. Her only suggestion was to speak to his brother Bill." I explained what she'd told me about his past and the circumstances in which "Brother Bill" lived as a retired man.

"Okay, so if Dave's death has nothing to do with anyone or anything that happened in Louisiana, why is she concerned that showing up in his life led to his death?"

"That's related, maybe, to the second conclusion I reached from our conversation. Meg is more concerned about Dave's relationship with associates here in California than any from his past. She asked me, pointblank, who Maggie could trust and raised concerns about several people in Dave's life. She didn't come right out and say it, but maybe she feels the trouble she and Maggie caused has to do with one of them."

"I've told you before, my love, until you have a solid lead on a suspect, everyone looks guilty. Tell me why Meg asked you that question." I did that, detailing our conversation, and set off a bout of the heebie-jeebies when I repeated Dave's lament that "people aren't always as they seem." Jack must have had a similar reaction.

"That does sound like Dave had stumbled into some trouble, doesn't it? You know Georgie, in his own clumsy way, Nick was just trying to keep Nora from getting herself killed." I heard a wistful tone in his voice as if he might be longing for the good old days when men like Nick Charles could lock up the woman he loved to keep her safe.

"I know that. I don't want some treacherous, two-faced rat in Dave's life to pen a requiescat in pace note for me. Come home soon."

"I will."

21 A BROTHER'S TALE

The next morning, I planned to call Bill using the phone number Pat had texted me. I was a little discouraged because along with Bill's phone number her text contained an answer to my question about Adam Middlemarch.

No tattoo that I've seen

"Do you think she's being dodgy again with her 'that I've seen' qualifier? Why can't she ever just give us a simple yes or no?"

"Don't worry. I plan to speak to Middlemarch again anyway. I'll have him show me his arms just to be on the safe side in case she's missed it."

"How could she miss something like that? He's a handyman, for goodness' sake. Are you telling me she's never seen his arms exposed while he was wearing a t-shirt or no shirt at all?"

"I can't answer that question, but I can tell you that whoever Emily ran into wasn't affiliated with Dave's security service. The service did a patrol by car around the time Dave arrived home, but no foot patrols."

"When did you have time to check with them?"

"There's lots of standing around time at a crime scene, especially while waiting for the CSIs to do their thing. I not only called the security service, but the limo company too. The limo driver was at the house a few minutes after the security patrol. He verified Emily's story that he dropped her off and then went back to pick her up less than fifteen minutes later."

"She did make a quick exit, didn't she? Did the limo driver see the security guard?"

"He saw someone, but only for a few seconds. A 'shadowy hulk' were his exact words. These limo drivers for the rich and famous talk like they're writing themselves into a movie script. No details—he wasn't even sure the figure was a man."

"I'm sorry. Maybe, you'll get something new from Emily that will help you figure out who she ran into. Or from questioning Adam if he was impersonating a security guard. Why he did that makes no sense, since he can come and go as he pleases in his handyman role."

"He was better off dressed as a security guard when he bumped into Emily than trying to explain why a handyman was roaming around the grounds after midnight."

"I'm sure you're right. That took forethought, don't you think? If he was in on the murder and mayhem Friday night, he planned to be there if he showed up in costume."

"True. Let's see what happens when I speak to him. Hank is trying to coordinate interviews with

Emily and Adam. It's a little trickier now that Emily's lawyer's involved. In the meantime, maybe the insurance adjuster will come through with the reports I've asked for or the CSIs will come up with something new from one of our crime scenes. We've got lots of irons in the fire, something's bound to move this investigation forward soon. Exciting, huh?" I got a big grin from my hale and hearty detective. When he left minutes later, he was whistling! How he does it, I'll never know, but it gave my spirits a boost. Or maybe it was the goodbye kiss that went with it.

As soon as I got to work, I called Bill Rollins and left a voice mail. I'd barely settled into my office when he returned my call.

"Way to go, Meg," I said as I picked up my cell phone.

Brother Bill had a quiet, even tone in his voice. I introduced myself, explained I was Dave's colleague, and helping to plan a company tribute to his brother. We chatted for a minute or two about his situation as a retired teacher who had become a member of the religious community on the grounds of the private school and served as a chaplain to local groups in the area. His voice bore more of a Southern Louisiana accent than Dave, Meg, or Maggie. Maybe he'd ditched some of those elocution lessons. I didn't ask. I did ask, as gently as I could, if he'd heard about the circumstance surrounding his brother's death.

"Yes. When Pat called to tell me he was dead, she also said the police were investigating his death. I understand he was murdered."

"As impossible as that is to believe."

"I don't find it impossible to believe at all. We're

both lucky we weren't killed long ago. Take too many chances, and your luck runs out before you get as old as Dave and me. Dave figured that out before I did, but that doesn't mean he'd wised up enough to stop taking risks altogether."

"Are you talking about the trouble he had in Louisiana when he became involved with Margaret Landry?"

"Yes, that's some of what I'm talking about," Bill replied wearily. "Nothing I ever did was for love like Dave. That's not to say he didn't live on the wild side for other reasons. We took pleasure in tormenting our parents by preferring friends who weren't from Louisiana's grand old families. That wasn't a sin. We met some good people. It was all the ratty stuff that went along with our unbridled rebellion. I thought Robert Landry's choice to be an outlaw was more authentic than our family's wretched heritage—which is old but not so grand as they'd have you believe. Eventually I saw firsthand where Landry's path led. Lots of people got hurt, like Dave. Some were even killed, like Robert."

"Hard lessons are often learned in a hard way," I offered, responding to the misery in Bill's voice.

"I've spent the past twenty years trying to make up for the hurt I caused. Dave's life took a turn for the better when he discovered music, and then, love. Good choices, although he didn't consider the consequences of ignoring the bond of matrimony. Especially when the bond Meg had made was to a man like Robert Landry. 'The heart wants what it wants,' to borrow an insight from Emily Dickinson."

"He gave her up."

"On some level he did—for her sake not his. There's an 'or else' with that Dickinson quote about the heart: 'or else it does not care.' I don't believe my brother ever cared about a woman in the same way again."

"You're not the first one to suggest that as a reason behind Dave's desperate pursuit of women. Even after Meg came back into his life and he learned that they shared a granddaughter, he didn't stop."

"True. In some ways when they reentered his life, he became more keenly aware of all he'd missed by leaving Louisiana and Meg behind."

"I don't see what choice he had. Even now, decades later, Meg's concerned she and Maggie may have had something to do with Dave's death."

"I don't believe there's anyone from Louisiana still out to get Dave or me. We both carried a load of guilt and plenty of damage from those old choices we made. In Dave's case, because he was never able to commit to a woman doesn't mean he didn't care about them. Too much, perhaps."

"Okay, can you explain what that means?"

"Dave called me a few weeks ago. 'Why is no one ever as they seem?' were the first words out of his mouth. He was obviously upset."

"Why?" I asked, recalling that, according to Meg, Dave had spoken almost the exact words to Maggie after a meeting with Skip and Jennifer.

"Someone was stealing from him. At first, it was small stuff, like a couple of gold medallions his boss had given him for an anniversary or a special occasion."

"I know them well. I sit on the Executive

Committee at Marvelous Marley World that commissioned a whole series of them over the years in his honor. They're lovely pieces that are worth more than the gold used to make them. Their value has to do with his notoriety, too."

"Whatever their value in a monetary sense, he expressed more distress about their sentimental value."

"I take it he didn't report this to the police?"

"No. He just let it go. Lately, though, he'd discovered what he believed to be theft on a bigger scale. A valuable item—a piece of original sheet music attributed to Mozart—turned up missing from among items he thought had been sent to the Marvelous Marley World archives. Then, a few days before he was killed, he discovered that a set of small art pieces he intended to hang in the hall upstairs was missing."

"No!" I gasped. A jumble of information Jack, and Carol, and I had discovered over the past few days tumbled through my mind. A sick, dizzy feeling crept over me.

"Did he tell you who was behind the thefts?"

"No. 'Someone close,' is all I could get him to tell me. He was more sad than angry, and unwilling to turn the matter over to the police even when he learned how big a loss he's suffered. He had plans to install video surveillance in his home and hired someone to do a new inventory of the art and collectibles kept in his home. He also intended to pay to have the items he'd sent to the archive cataloged, so he'd have a better idea of what all was missing. I'm certain he hoped all the new scrutiny would discourage the person who was stealing from him."

"He must have felt awful about having to resort to such efforts."

"We've spent most of our old age feeling awful, usually about how many people we hurt. It's also been discouraging to learn how many people there are in the world with no better values than the ones we possessed when we were younger. I wish I'd tried harder to get him to go to the police, maybe he'd still be alive."

"I hope you're not blaming yourself. Dave has never been shy in the past about using the legal system to seek justice. He was protecting someone. I doubt anything you could have said would have changed his mind. Besides, I have it on very good authority that the only one to blame for a crime is the person who commits it."

"I'll try to hang onto that idea when I watch them bury my brother. I'm flying out tomorrow for his funeral even though I dread having to face Dave's ex-wife. Not very charitable of me, is it? I tried to talk some sense into Dave about her, but he believed in the old 'keep your friends close and your enemies closer.' I heard Robert Landry say that once, too, not long before friends who were also enemies killed him."

"Do you think Dave was speaking about her when he said someone close?"

"It could be. To be perfectly honest with you, I couldn't ever quite figure out if she was friend or foe. Meg said you're putting a memorial together for my brother at Marvelous Marley World. I'd like to join you."

"That would be wonderful! Would you be willing

to deliver a benediction at the start of the event?"

"Sure. It's the least I can do. My brother bailed me out, literally, when I got into legal trouble and paid to hire lawyers who put those troubles behind me. Then he set me up with a new life, that included changing my name to Rollins, like his, and getting an education. Despite his weaknesses, my brother was a talented man who yearned for decency."

"I suppose that's about the best any of us can do, isn't it?" The moment I hung up the phone, I called Jack.

"Isn't that interesting?" Jack commented once I'd shared Bill's story. "I wonder who he was protecting? Here's another bit of news for you. Would it surprise you to hear Pat went to dinner with the insurance adjuster?"

"No!"

"Yep. They've been friends for years, according to Roger Winters, and recently began seeing each other."

"How did you get him to tell you that?"

"I called him to find out when we could get our hands on the reports he's putting together. Then I asked how he ended up at Dave's estate as quick as he did and on a Sunday. He told me he'd done it because Pat was so upset at dinner the night before. That's when he spilled the beans about their budding romance."

"Well, if Pat was stealing from Dave, having Roger Winters eating out of the palm of her hand was clever. She claimed sending in the packing and storage team was Jennifer's idea. Did Pat make that up?"

"Oh, no, that was Jennifer's doing. Remember

the passing remark she made about the redesign of Dave's beach cottage putting her in touch with her 'artsy' side?"

"Yes," I replied.

"She was speaking the truth. Her major in college was art history. Before she trained as an accountant, she worked as an art appraiser."

"Wow, I'm sure she must have been a real asset to Dave in his selection of art and collectibles." There was a note of sarcasm in my voice, since I wasn't sure how much help she might have been. Art appraisal is tricky and it's not uncommon for buyers to pay more than they should if they're fed misinformation about the provenance or market value of a piece.

"But wait! There's more! One of her old colleagues from her 'artsy' days happens to be an appraiser with the packing and storage company she sent out there on Sunday. The owner tells me they've handled Dave's artwork for years and the 'usual appraiser' would update the value of his holdings as part of an inventory Dave ordered recently. Did you know guys like Dave rotate art pieces throughout the year?" Jack asked.

"Sure, if the collection is too large for all of it to be displayed at once. That past association between Jennifer and her appraiser better be disclosed on whatever form the firm has employees fill out about potential conflicts of interest. If not, she could have some explaining to do."

"I'm going to sound like a copycat, now, but if Jennifer was stealing from Dave, having the appraiser eating out of the palm of her hand was clever. Remember when I promised to have another Q & A session with her? It's time! I'll set up an appointment at her office tomorrow. Then I'm going to track down Pat Dolan and ask her why she didn't say anything to us about the missing medallions even if they went missing before the break-in."

"That Pat or Jennifer would do such a thing makes me sick. I even kind of wish they shared Marla's self-serving psychopathic ability to see the virtue in not killing the golden goose."

"Avarice often gets the best of people, especially if they feel aggrieved about what they regard as an old injustice like being dumped by the maestro. I wouldn't rule Marla out yet."

"If the thief got wind of Dave's plans to make it more difficult to steal from him and feared he was going to call in the authorities, I suppose killing the goose that laid the golden egg was preferable to prison."

22 BEGGING TO BE CAUGHT

You never can tell where you'll get the break you need to solve a crime. As much emphasis as there is on forensic evidence like DNA, fingerprints, or trace material transferred at the time the crime occurred, it's more often human character that tells the tale. Maybe, the culprit can't keep the dirty deed a secret, confides in someone or boasts about it in public or private, and the wrong person overhears it. Or there's a falling out between lovers or friends, or among co-conspirators. Liars never can keep their stories straight. Alibis disappear, or bad guys lose what little hold they have left on anything normal and act out as if begging to be caught. The end of the line for Dave's killer came about in just such a way.

Our morning had started off steeped in murder and mayhem. Jack had that "cat that swallowed the canary" look on his face as he headed out the door to the Lost Hills police station first thing. Hank had finally arranged to bring Adam Middlemarch in for a sit down around the same time Emily Lombard was scheduled to have her interview. He'd planned to make sure their paths crossed. Then Jack was off to LA for his Q & A session with Jennifer Wainwright.

"Things are about to happen, sweetheart. I can feel it in my old detective bones."

"Vintage, darling, not old. Take care of them, will you? I've grown quite fond of them. Jennifer Wainwright is a wily dame if there ever was one! Ruthless, too, if she's the mastermind behind theft, two murders, assault, and who knows what else. Yesterday, I told Meg to hire a good lawyer for Maggie in case there's something dicey about Dave's will."

When I called Jack from my office later, he wasn't as upbeat after learning that Adam had no tattoo of any kind on his arm. Emily Lombard wasn't much help either when it came to identifying Adam as the guy she'd seen Friday night on Dave's property. He was about the right size, but in the dark hadn't seen his face clearly enough to say Adam was the same man. Disappointing news, but I had a tidbit that would lift his spirits.

"Carol says it's Jennifer wearing those gold loop earrings at the gala. She'll text you a copy of photos she's found if you want them."

"Are you sure?" I thought my detective pal was on the verge of a woohoo by the surge of enthusiasm in his voice.

"Carol also tells me she dug up a picture or two where Jennifer and Dave are out on the town together. No one ever pegged them as a couple, but the body language says more than colleagues to me. Do you want those pictures for your chat with

Jennifer?"

"Please. Have Carol send them all to me right away. My chat may not be a very long one, however, given that Jennifer works in a building full of attorneys. It won't surprise me if she lawyers up quick. I'm going to bring her down to the police station for questioning if that happens. Jennifer has another problem."

"Besides her friendship with an art appraiser who's a corporate vendor?"

"Yes. She got a parking ticket Friday night, after midnight, on Pacific Coast Highway. The location is within walking distance of the maestro's estate."

"No! That's three strikes, isn't it: the old friend who poses a conflict of interest, the earring found in Dave's office, and a parking ticket that puts her near the scene on the night he was killed?"

"Yes, but it's too soon to count her out. I have a search warrant and an order to seize the property in storage. I want an independent review of Dave's artwork and collections to determine what's missing. In the meantime, we'll see what Skip has to say once we ask him why he lied for his colleague."

"He did say they went somewhere for a nightcap with folks they ran into at the gala."

"Yes. Here's another part of the lifestyles of the rich and famous you never told me about—afterparties."

"We were invited. To more than one, in fact. It never occurred to me that you'd want to go," I said. "I've figured you're a one-party-a-night fellow, especially when the parties involve Max and his Marvelous Marley World minions."

"If I had my way, I'd be a no-party-a-night fellow, especially when it comes to Max and his minions. The party I'm talking about was hosted by the Mirador Hotel. There's no way Jennifer was in Santa Monica with her chums based on the time that parking ticket was issued. When we followed up with them, not only Skip, but Adam claimed to have gone to that party."

"Can they prove it?"

"Skip left a trail that puts him at the party until dawn—well past the time Dave was killed. Adam's name was on an invitation list, and he checked in early. A little before the gala ended, in fact. He never picked up a bag of swag that was in a room opened to invited guests a little later. I can't imagine a guy like Adam turning down free stuff, can you?"

"Not unless he left before the Gift Lounge opened. He missed a chance to cash in on some real loot. I donated our swag to a local charity, by the way. I'll bet that's what Jennifer did, too, didn't she?"

"We had swag? I missed loot? Good loot?"

"Excellent. Max put us on the A-list," I replied. "Why would a struggling handyman miss out on a chance to get free Bluetooth headphones and wireless speakers among other gifts?"

"I'll have to ask him that. It's a good thing he's still being kept comfortable at the Lost Hills station, isn't it?"

"I guess so. My head is spinning! So much is happening so fast, isn't it? Remind me never to doubt your old bones."

"Vintage, not old," was all he could say before my phone rang. My cell phone, not my office phone.

"Hang on, Jack. I've got a call."

"Answer it. You're right about how much is happening. I'd better get to it. I'll call you later." I'm not sure if he even heard me say goodbye before he hung up. When my phone rang for the third time, I finally picked up the call.

"Georgie, it's Pat."

"Hi, Pat. What is it?"

"I'm at Dave's place. I've found something on Dave's computer I think you and Jack should see."

"Jack's going to be tied up for a while, but I'll tell him to come and join us as soon as he can."

"It's not an emergency, and I have a realtor dropping by, so no rush. I just wanted to catch you as soon as possible so you could head north to Malibu before the rush hour madness settles in this afternoon."

"That's a good idea. I have good news for you from Bill Rollins. I'll tell you all about my chat with him when I get there."

Well, not all of it, I thought, biting my bottom lip. I wasn't going to reveal the doubts both Bill and Meg had expressed about Pat's trustworthiness considering what Jack had learned today about Jennifer. In fact, I wasn't sure I should say much of anything to Pat about today's revelations until Jack had put more of the puzzle together. It might even be a good idea to wait until he or the Lost Hills police made an arrest.

Carol, who was staring at me, owllike, with big round eyes, was a different story. She knew something was up, immediately.

"Jack says thanks for the picture of Jennifer in those earrings. He's on his way to pick her up for questioning. Her sidekick, Skip, too. While he rounds them up, I'm heading out to Dave's place to meet with Pat. I've left a message for Jack to meet me there."

"Cool! It sounds like Rockford is about to blow this case wide open."

"Let's keep a low profile about this for a while longer. Our detective friend has a few hurdles to jump before he can close the book on the murder of the maestro." I sighed as a wave of sadness hit about Dave's death. Carol and I had already gone another round of planning for the memorial service.

The moment I got to Dave's house, I felt things weren't right. I should have listened to the echo of Mile's booming voice bouncing around in my head. The gate was open, so I drove right in. Pat's car was already parked in the circular drive. A realtor's car was parked behind hers. I rang the doorbell, but no one answered. I knocked and that didn't get a response, either. Growing more uncomfortable by the minute, I decided to leave.

Then, I heard Pat's voice coming from the patio around back. She was either speaking to someone on her phone or to that realtor. A huge wave of relief hit me. If she was outside and engaged in a conversation, maybe she didn't hear me knock or ring the doorbell.

As I walked around the side of the house, Pat's voice grew louder, although I couldn't make out what she and the person with her were discussing. It must have been important since there was an urgency about it. I didn't want to eavesdrop, so as I came around the corner I called out.

"Hey, Pat! It's Georgie, I…" What I saw,

stopped me in my tracks. "Oh no! What are you doing?" Pat was sort of straddling the white railing that ran around the edge of the veranda. It looked nautical, like that on the ship Jack and I took on our all-too-eventful honeymoon cruise. One leg dangled half over the edge of the rail. Her other leg was still on a chair pushed against it. The pose screamed suicide. I screamed for her to stop!

"Don't do it! Whatever's going on, we'll deal with it." I took a few steps onto the veranda, not wanting to startle Pat by moving toward her too quickly.

"What are you doing here?" A woman asked as she stood, hidden in the shadow of the patio cover. She pointed a gun at Pat. The body of another woman lay in a heap at her feet. I recognized the woman's voice even before I could see her face when she stepped forward and pointed the gun at me.

"That was going to be my question to you, Connie." I spoke in a soft, calm tone trying not to antagonize the obviously distressed woman. Her hand shook as she held that gun.

"You picked the wrong time to butt in, you, meddlesome fool!" The chair on which Pat still had one foot squeaked a little. Connie turned the gun back on her.

"Don't you dare get down. This is all your fault. If you had an ounce of decency, you would have put an end to Dave's lechery long ago."

"How did you expect her to do that?" I asked softly. The gun moved again, back toward me, and then toward Pat, before finally settling on a point somewhere in between that meant neither of us was staring down the barrel of a gun.

"I don't know," she said, looking down at the gun in her hand. "Someone had to stop him from hurting more women. My niece had no idea what heartache she faced. I tried to tell her not to get mixed up with him."

"That must have worked since she left Friday night, right?" The gun dropped a little lower. Connie nodded and began to weep.

"I didn't know that. When Dave came swaggering by on the trail he was wearing that horrid velvet jacket. I heard someone coming and figured it was Emily on her way to meet him. That's when I picked up a stick and hit him." The gun she held moved up and down as if she had that stick in her hand. "I didn't mean to hit him as hard as I did. He fell. I threw that stick away and ran." As she said that, she tossed the gun into the swimming pool and sank to the ground. The injured woman moved.

"It's okay, Connie. I believe you," I said as I dialed 911 calling for an ambulance.

"Me, too," Pat said suddenly standing at my side.

23 CODA

"Connie's made a full confession. She's facing a second-degree murder charge. Her lawyer might get that reduced to manslaughter if they believe her claim that she didn't intend to kill the maestro."

"What a tragedy," Pat added. "I'm not sure what I would have done if Roger Winters had turned out to be part of Jennifer Wainwright's scheme. I suppose we both looked guilty, didn't we?" Jack didn't respond, so I did.

"Jack has told me more than once, 'until you have a solid lead on a suspect, everyone looks guilty.' When we met, I was suspect number one until he determined that my alibi was fool-proof. Here's to us, and the relief that goes with being ex-suspects!" I raised my glass to Pat who gave it a little clink.

"Neither of you were ever officially suspects, although you both came close. I'm glad you're both in such good spirits after the close call you had." Jack raised his glass. "Here's to me, too, for not having a heart attack when Hank called to tell me he was on his way to Dave Rollins' house where an incident had taken place that required an ambulance." We clinked his glass.

"At least I didn't keep you in suspense for long. I texted you that Pat and I were okay as soon as I could clear my head enough to do it."

"Well I've had enough suspense to last a lifetime," Pat added. "It's a good thing you showed up when you did, Georgie, or we wouldn't be having dinner on your terrace. There's no way I could have jumped, so Connie probably would have shot me."

"Shooting you wouldn't have convinced anyone that you'd committed suicide. Even with the neatly typed note she left in Dave's house proclaiming your sorrow and guilt for murdering the maestro," I said. "Connie should have scuttled her plan the minute the realtor saw her with a gun. By the time I arrived, she didn't need much coaxing to let it go."

"She's lucky not to be facing two murder charges after hitting that realtor as hard as she did," Jack asserted. "I hate it when hapless bystanders wander into the middle of a crazy scheme as it's unraveling. The realtor's going to be okay, but poor Charlie won't get another chance."

"Requiescat in pace," I said.

"I don't know if I qualify as a hapless bystander, but I'm grateful I didn't get pulled into a violent confrontation with Adam working as Jennifer's inside man. He's a bigger disappointment to me than Connie. Dave hurt her deeply, but he did a lot for that stupid, ungrateful jerk. Did Adam tell you Dave paid for his singing lessons and community college tuition?

That's in addition to the money he gave him for his work as a handyman."

"For some people, it's never enough. Adam's doing his best to get charges reduced or dropped in exchange for testifying against Jennifer. He's savvier than he seems. One of Adam's first jobs was as an assistant to a bail bondsman. That's where he picked up his sneaky, eavesdropping skills and learned a few things about how to act when lawyers ask you questions. Even when he was younger, he was big enough to make a go of it as a skip chaser except that he got jumped. When it's two on one, it doesn't matter so much that you're the biggest guy in the room. That painful incident changed his mind, and he took a job in maintenance at Marvelous Marley World."

"His sneaking around got him into more hot water than he could handle when he caught Jennifer red-handed and cut himself in for a piece of the action."

"True, but the real trouble started when Dave called the vendor he'd always used and made arrangements for an unscheduled audit of his holdings. Jennifer's appraiser pal called her right away. Adam says she was panicky and kept telling him 'they' needed to do something quick or he'd be in as much trouble as she was. Like the dumb crooks that they were, she and Adam dug a deeper hole and jumped in it. Jennifer planned to get into Dave's house, trash the place, and make it look as if a thief had been searching for something specific like those missing letters written to Dave by a would-be Mozart."

"A thief with an ax to grind and an interest in

Mozart," I said. "It sure eventually looked as though that letter-writing culprit was responsible for the break-in, vandalism, and even murder, especially when all the wolfman, big 'M' stuff started up again."

"I helped them pull that off, didn't I, by sending you on the Wolf Gang wild goose chase?"

"That's what they hoped would happen. Dave was supposed to come back from his moonlit stroll to the vandalism, discover the missing letters, and report it to the police," Jack said.

"When we met with Skip and Jennifer at their office, she told us you were the 'keeper of the Mozart letters.' In a way, we ended up prodding you to discover those letters were missing that Jennifer hoped would establish the presence in the house of someone interested in stealing them," I added.

"Dave's murder changed their plan. In all the disorder and confusion, Jennifer ordered the art and collectibles moved into storage."

"Dave sure contributed to the confusion by not confiding in you about the missing medallions or the art pieces that had disappeared," I added.

"He outright lied to me when he said he'd donated the missing medallions to USC. I didn't even know about the art pieces Jennifer had stolen. Roger says Dave added them to the inventory when he purchased them, but no one ever saw them. It's hard to tell the police there's been a theft when the owner has covered it up." Pat shrugged.

"If Jennifer had just kept her cool, it sounds as if she could have gotten away with it. Why attack us on Sunday?"

"Max called Jennifer and ordered her to

cooperate with us fully. He claimed you and Dave had been close friends for years and he expected you to be able to get to the bottom of things in no time flat. She must have figured you were onto something when you decided to return so soon for another look around. Your talent for snooping is becoming well-known."

"Yeah, right. Connie had a different term for it—meddlesome fool's more her take on my talent. Given the way Max had been singing your praises as a lawman, I bet that rock throwing was more about stopping you than me. Either way, she succeeded in slowing us down long enough to get Dave's art and collectibles out of the house and into storage."

"Adam claims he believed Jennifer was going to cover up their thievery by putting the stolen items in with those moved into storage," Jack said.

"If she still had his property, it wasn't about the money, was it?" Pat asked. "It's as if she wanted to steal pieces of Dave's life he wasn't willing or able to give her."

"It could be. Skip hasn't said much, apart from claiming he originally backed up Jennifer's alibi because he didn't know she'd left the party. He admitted that Jennifer was upset when she found out Dave intended to leave that cottage to you, Pat. She was furious, too, when he made all sorts of provisions in his will for a granddaughter he didn't even know."

"Has Hank recovered the stolen goods from the storage facility?"

"No. He found them, though—all packed up in a carry-on bag in the trunk of Jennifer's car."

"What a liar!" Pat exclaimed. "She was going to

run, wasn't she?"

"Running makes more sense if she killed Charlie. She couldn't just make that go away, could she?"

"Sad, but true. Unfortunately, Charlie was doomed once he bumped into Adam. Adam had already been out on the trail looking for Jennifer's missing earring with that backpack and the metal detector. She thought she lost it on the trail Friday night walking from her car to Dave's house before she trashed the place. She sent Adam to search for it early Sunday morning."

"Jennifer must have nearly passed out when you showed her the earring and that photo of her wearing it Friday night." Jack shook his head at that comment as if he couldn't believe what he'd seen.

"She turned a lighter shade of white than that wig Adam wore as part of his wolfman disguise. Adam put that on when Jennifer sent him back out to the trail to stop us. I don't believe it mattered to her if he injured us in the process or not, but Adam assured me he missed us on purpose."

"I take it that wolfman getup was more of their attempt to sell the idea that a mad Mozart was on the loose," Pat commented.

"Yes. Adam hoped we'd see him and report we'd been attacked by some crazy guy with white hair under his hoodie and wearing a Wolf Gang t-shirt. We didn't get a good enough look at him, but Charlie did. Poor Charlie had two problems. One that he wasn't all there, and two, that he'd met Adam before. Jennifer panicked again, convinced that Charlie would eventually tell the police about Adam and lead them back to her. Adam swears he told her she didn't have to worry about it, that he'd disguised his face and voice, and added padding to his body so that Charlie couldn't recognize him. She didn't believe Adam after he assured her he'd spoken to Charlie with the police standing right there and the guy hadn't identified him."

"So, what happened?"

"Adam's holding onto that card while he plays 'let's make a deal.' We have Jennifer's car which she must have used to move Charlie to Crystal Cove. She paid to have it cleaned the day after we found Charlie's body. There's still a good chance we'll get something that puts Charlie in her car and pins his murder on Jennifer even without Adam's testimony. As a teaser, Adam told us she was looking for Charlie to 'pay him off' so he'd keep his mouth shut. I'm betting that Adam's hesitation about spilling the beans before he gets a deal is that he helped Jennifer figure out where to find Charlie. Accessory to murder may be in the cards for Adam Middlemarch."

"What a tragic set of circumstances converged on that Friday night!" I declared sadly.

"You could blame it on the full moon except that Jennifer's dirty work began long before that and continued after that night when she tracked Charlie down and killed him. Adam's betrayal, too," Pat added.

"Some of those circumstances were set in motion long ago, weren't they?" Jack asked.

"That's so true. Meg's hunch that their re-entry into Dave's life led to his death was partly correct since his generosity toward Maggie helped push Jennifer over the edge. Dave's compulsive pursuit of women pulled Emily and Connie into situations in which they should never have become involved. Connie's inability to let go of the past set her up to make the worst mistake of her life. Emily's going to have to deal with that mistake, too."

"At least we'll be able to celebrate Dave's life without the murder of the maestro hovering around us as a mystery still to be solved. That's something, isn't it?" Pat asked, trying to brighten the sadness that had settled on us.

"True, except that we still have to face Max before then. He wants 'to be filled in completely before he stands up for his friend and reports to the Marvelous Marley World family that justice has been served.'"

"We?" Jack asked.

"Oh, yes, Sir Jack of Crystal Cove. I'm counting on you." I tried not to take it as a bad omen when Miles bellowed from where he sat peering at us through the screen door.

"It's okay, Miles. I was only teasing. I won't let St. Joan face that dragon alone."

As I explained our silliness about knights and saints to Pat, Jack went inside. In less than a minute, music engulfed us. Swept up in *A Little Night Music*, we listened to that song from Dave's *Mozart Meets Jazz* album Pat brought us as a gift. We fell silent. What more could we say about the maestro and his music? Where words fail, music speaks.

THE END

Thanks for reading *Murder of the Maestro Georgie*

Shaw Cozy Mystery #6. Please, please, please take a minute and leave me a review on Amazon and Goodreads. I'd love to get your feedback! Your reviews matter so much to readers and to me. Thank you!

I hope if you're not already signed up for my newsletter that you'll drop by my website at http://desertcitiesmystery.com. Sign up to get updates about new releases, sales, and giveaways. New subscribers get a FREE eBook. While you're there, feel free to leave a comment or ask a question!

To find the rest of the books in this series and books in other series I write, follow me on Amazon @ https://www.amazon.com/Anna-Celeste-Burke/e/B00H8J4IQS

What's up next for Georgie and Jack?

In *A Tango Before Dying Georgie Shaw Cozy Mystery #7*, murder and mayhem come waltzing into Georgie and Jack's life.

Georgie's Executive Assistant, Carol Ripley, is understandably upset when she learns that her godmother and namesake, Madame Carol Chantel, is dead she's understandably upset. Her death comes as a surprise since the beloved dance teacher and well-known Ballroom Dance Champion was in excellent health. It's even more shocking when the Santa Barbara police report her death as suspicious, and an autopsy reveals someone murdered Madame Chantel.

In the immortal words of Voltaire, "Let us read, and let us dance; these two amusements will never do any harm to the world." Reading maybe, but not dance, apparently. Dressed as she was when the police found her body, a tango before dying was Madame Chantel's final act.

Carol implores Georgie Shaw and Detective Jack Wheeler to find out who killed her godmother. Was it a jealous romantic partner, a rival in the competitive world of Ballroom Dancing, an overly friendly neighbor, a dispute with a local businesswoman, or someone else who murdered Madame Chantel? Look for your copy later in 2018.

RECIPES

Chicken Marsala
Serves 4

Ingredients
1/4 cup all-purpose flour
1/2 teaspoon salt
1/4 teaspoon ground black pepper
1/2 teaspoon dried oregano
4 skinless, boneless chicken breast halves - pounded
1/4 inch thick
4 tablespoons butter
4 tablespoons olive oil
1 cup sliced cremini mushrooms
3 ounces shitake mushrooms
1/2 cup Marsala wine

Directions

1. In a shallow dish or bowl, mix together the flour, salt, pepper and oregano. Coat chicken pieces in flour mixture.

2. In a large skillet, melt butter in oil over medium heat. Place chicken in the pan, and lightly brown. Turn over chicken pieces and add mushrooms. Pour in wine and sherry. Cover skillet; simmer chicken 10 minutes, turning once, until no longer pink and juices run clear.

Georgie's Tips

It's hard to find a simpler dish that's as delicious as this one. It sounds a little exotic and is fancy enough to serve guests. Because it's so easy and tasty, you won't want to wait until you have company to fix it.

Serve this dish with some crusty bread and a starchy side dish that will let you enjoy every bit of the sauce that makes this chicken so scrumptious. Fresh linguini as I do in the maestro's story. Delicious when tossed in olive oil and fresh garlic. Or creamy mashed potatoes, like those made with the recipe that follows. A simple risotto, noodles or another pasta will work, too.

Add a side salad or a brightly colored vegetable, like fresh green beans, carrots, or broccoli and you have all your basic food groups covered...except for chocolate, of course! Check out the brownie recipe to finish out this wonderful meal.

Creamy Mashed Potatoes
6 Servings

Ingredients
2 Pounds Idaho potatoes
3 Tablespoons salted butter
4 Ounces cream cheese
1 Cup whole milk
Salt & pepper to taste

Directions

1. Peel potatoes and rinse them. Cut into even sized pieces and place into a large pot. Cover with water and add a dash of salt. Bring to boil, then reduce to simmer. Cook until fork tender, about 20 minutes. Drain completely and place potatoes back into the hot pot.

2. Mash potatoes with butter, cream cheese, milk, salt and pepper until desired consistency has been reached. Delicious served warm with butter or gravy.

Georgie's Tips

These are a perfect accompaniment to Marsala Chicken. You can place the chicken right on top the mashed potatoes letting the sauce serve as the gravy. Or, place the chicken off to one side and drizzle with the Marsala sauce.

Want to turn these into garlic mashed potatoes? Crush two or three cloves of garlic and along with the other ingredients.

Chocolate Mascarpone Brownies
16 brownies

Ingredients
Brownies
1 cup unsalted butter
3 ounces semi-sweet chocolate, chopped
1 cup granulated white sugar
1/2 cup unsweetened cocoa powder
1/2 cup mascarpone cheese, at room temperature
3 large, at room temperature eggs
2 teaspoons vanilla extract
1/2 cup all-purpose flour
1/4 teaspoon salt
Ganache
6 ounces semi-sweet chocolate, finely chopped
6 Tablespoons whipping cream
3 Tablespoons unsalted butter

Directions
1. Preheat oven to 325°F. Butter an 8-inch square pan.

2. Place chopped chocolate in a mixing bowl; set aside. In a small glass bowl, melt butter in microwave, just until melted- don't let it cook and bubble. Pour butter over the chocolate and let stand for 30 seconds. Stir until chocolate is completely melted and butter is well incorporated. Sift in sugar and cocoa powder.

3. With a wooden spoon, beat in mascarpone, eggs and vanilla, mixing until smooth. Gently fold in flour and salt.

4. Pour batter into prepared pan and spread evenly. Place into preheated oven and bake 45 to 50 minutes, or until a tester comes out clean.

5. Place pan on cooling rack and let brownies cool 10 to 15 minutes while you make the ganache.

6. Place chopped chocolate in a mixing bowl. In a small saucepan, bring the cream and butter to just below boiling point, over medium heat. Pour this hot mixture over the chocolate and let stand for 30 seconds, then stir until smooth. Pour ganache over brownies while still warm and spread to cover evenly.

7. Let ganache firm up before cutting. It's best to refrigerate them until quite firm. Once the ganache is firm and the brownies have been cut, they do not need to be kept in the refrigerator.

White Bean Soup
4-6 servings

Ingredients
1/2 cup dry white wine

2 sprigs fresh rosemary, each about 6 inches long

2 sprigs fresh thyme

2 1/2 cups low-sodium chicken or vegetable broth

Two 15-ounce cans of cannellini or other white beans, strained and rinsed

1 small shallot, peeled, trimmed and halved

1 small garlic clove, peeled, trimmed and halved

1 tablespoon olive oil

1 tablespoon unsalted butter

Kosher salt and freshly ground black pepper

Directions
1. Bring the wine, rosemary, thyme and 2 cups of the chicken broth to a boil in a covered medium saucepan over high heat. Reduce to a bare simmer.

2. Puree the beans, shallots, garlic, oil, butter, remaining 1/2 cup chicken broth, 1/2 teaspoon salt, a few grinds of pepper and 1/2 cup of the simmering broth in a blender until completely smooth and emulsified, about 2 minutes.

3. Remove the herb sprigs from the simmering broth; set aside. Whisk the bean puree into the broth and return it to a gentle boil.

4. Ladle the soup into bowls, and garnish with the reserved herb sprigs and a few grinds of black pepper.

Sole Meunière
4 Servings

Ingredients

½ cup all-purpose flour

6 4-ounce skinless, boneless sole or other thin fish fillets, patted dry

Kosher salt, to taste

Freshly ground white or black pepper, to taste

4 tablespoons clarified butter

4 tablespoons unsalted butter, diced, at room temperature

3 tablespoons minced parsley

1 lemon, cut into wedges, for garnish

Directions

1. Heat oven to 200 degrees and place a large oven-safe plate or baking sheet inside.

2. Place flour on a large, shallow plate. Season both sides of fish fillets with salt and pepper to taste. Dredge fish in flour, shaking off excess.

3. In a 12-inch nonstick or enamel-lined skillet over medium-high heat, heat 2 tablespoons clarified butter until bubbling. Place half of the fish fillets in the pan and cook until just done, 2 to 3 minutes per side, then transfer to the plate or baking sheet in the oven to keep warm. Add 2 more tablespoons clarified butter to skillet and heat until bubbling, then cook remaining fillets. Wipe out the skillet.

4. Arrange the fish on a warm serving platter. Top with parsley. In reserved skillet, heat remaining 4 tablespoons unsalted butter until bubbling and

golden, 1 to 2 minutes, then pour evenly over fillets. Serve immediately, with lemon wedges on the side.

Georgie's Tips

Sole Meunière is a fast and easy meal to prepare. However, the recipe does call for clarified butter, butter that has had the milk solids and water removed, which can be made in advance. The reason clarified butter is so important in this recipe, and others that require heating butter over high heat, is that by removing the milk solids and water you can cook at a higher heat without burning the butter or causing it to smoke.

This Sole Meunière recipe requires 5-6 tablespoons of clarified butter. When you make clarified butter, you lose about a quarter of the butter you started with. For this recipe start with 8 tablespoons (1 stick) butter to end up with 6 tablespoons clarified butter. You can also make a larger quantity than what's needed for this recipe because clarified butter keeps well.

How to Make Clarified Butter

To make clarified butter, you place the butter in a small saucepan and heat over low heat. As the butter heats up, it will begin to separate into three layers. Foam will form on the top, the clarified butter will be in the center, and the milk solids will be on the bottom of the pan. Skim the foam off (you can save this for later, if you want to use it in other dishes). Line a sieve with cheesecloth and strain the remaining butter in the saucepan, leaving the solids in the pan.

Roasted Herbed Baby Potatoes
4-6 servings

Ingredients
1-pound mixed baby potatoes—white, purple, & red
1 Tablespoon Herbs de Provence
¼ Cup First Cold Pressed EVOO
2 Cloves Garlic, chopped
Salt & Pepper to taste

Directions
1. Preheat oven to 400°F. Put the potatoes into a large bowl.
2. In a small bowl, whisk the herbs, garlic, and oil together until blended. Pour over the potatoes. Sprinkle generously with salt and pepper, then toss to coat.
3. Transfer the potatoes to a large heavy baking dish, spacing them evenly apart. Roast the potatoes until they are tender and golden, turning them occasionally with tongs for 45 minutes.

Georgie's Tips
Baby potatoes and new potatoes are similar, but not exactly the same. Some people call any small potato a new potato, but new potatoes differ from baby potatoes in that they have been freshly dug up and brought to the grocery store without curing. Most potatoes you buy in a store have been stored for a couple weeks, during which time they are cured to set the peel and heal any cuts or nicks in the skin, which makes the potatoes last longer. Because new potatoes skip this step, they are usually more moist and sweeter than other small potatoes.

Not all olive oil is created equal. Some olive oils are diluted with soybean oil, which lowers the quality and the potential health benefits in olive oil. First cold-pressed, extra virgin olive oil [EVOO]
This combination of white, red, and purple baby potatoes makes this dish look extra special, but the dish will taste as good whatever color potatoes you use. Fingerling
In hurry? You can cut the potatoes in half before tossing them in the coating and roast them in about 20-30 minutes.

Herbs de Provence—buy a delightful blend of herbs or make it for yourself!
Herbs de Provence is a mixture of dried herbs typical of the Provence region of southeast France often used with grilled foods and stews. There's no standard recipe for this blend, so if commercial blends may vary. Many chefs make their own since it's easy to do using whatever combination of herbs they enjoy. Most versions will contain marjoram, thyme, rosemary, and oregano plus some combination of others. I think a hint or mint and lavender make the blend special. Here's a starter recipe for you, but experiment until you find the perfect version for you. In a pretty, air-tight container, your personalized version would make a lovely gift for a family member or friend who loves to cook.

Ingredients
4 tablespoons thyme 3 tablespoons marjoram 3 tablespoons summer savory 2 tablespoon rosemary 1 tablespoon tarragon 1 tablespoon basil 1 tablespoon fennel seeds 1 teaspoon mint 1 teaspoon chervil 1

teaspoon mint 1 teaspoon lavender

Directions

Grind rosemary and fennel seed in a spice grinder; transfer to a mixing bowl. Stir savory, thyme, basil, marjoram, lavender, parsley, oregano, tarragon, and bay powder with the rosemary and fennel. Store in an air-tight container between uses.

Sautéed Baby Vegetables
4 servings

Ingredients
1 pound assorted mini squash - patty pans and/or baby zucchini
3 tablespoons extra-virgin olive oil
1 cup frozen pearl onions
1 pint cherry tomatoes
Salt and freshly ground black pepper
3 to 4 tablespoons chopped fresh dill Handful flat-leaf parsley, chopped

Directions
1. Halve the squash. Heat the extra-virgin olive oil in a large skillet over medium-high heat.

2. Sauté the squash 5 minutes then add the onions and tomatoes, season the vegetables with salt and pepper and cook 5 to 7 minutes more until the tomatoes begin to burst and the onions are warmed through. Toss the herbs with the vegetables and transfer to a serving dish.

Georgie's Tips
Baby vegetables are tender and delicious. There's also something elegant about the way they look on a plate. I find this mini squash combo prepackaged in several local grocery stores. There's nothing that says you must use this combination of veggies with all the options baby carrots or brussels sprouts, button mushrooms, baby eggplant, baby beets, or haricot vert, a French green bean that's tiny. Try different

combos for variety in taste, nutrition, and presentation.

When they're available at the market and I have time, I prefer using fresh pearl onions, sometimes available in red, yellow, and white colors.

Chewy Oatmeal Chocolate Chip Cookies
Makes 3 ½ dozen cookies

Ingredients
1 cup butter, softened
1 cup packed light brown sugar
1/2 cup white sugar
2 eggs
2 teaspoons vanilla extract
1 1/4 cups all-purpose flour
1/2 teaspoon baking soda
1 teaspoon salt
3 cups old-fashioned rolled oats
1 cup chopped pecans
1 cup semisweet chocolate chips

Directions
1. Preheat the oven to 325 degrees F (165 degrees C).

2. In a large bowl, cream together the butter, brown sugar, and white sugar until smooth. Beat in eggs one at a time, then stir in vanilla. Combine the flour, baking soda, and salt; stir into the creamed mixture until just blended. Mix in the quick oats, walnuts, and chocolate chips. Drop by the heaping spoonful onto ungreased baking sheets.

3. Bake for 12 minutes in the preheated oven. Allow cookies to cool on baking sheet for 5 minutes before transferring to a wire rack to cool completely.

Georgie's Tips
These cookies are comfort food! Easy to make and

quick to bake, they store well, and are easy to pack and carry for lunches or parties. I prefer the old-fashioned rolled oats, but quick oats will work, too. Choose another variety of nuts if you're not a fan of pecans or leave them out altogether. Enjoy!

Shepherd's Pie with a Pastry Crust
Serves 6

Ingredients
1 pre-made deep dish pie shell
3/4 pound ground beef, lamb, or turkey
1 medium onion
2 garlic cloves, chopped
8 ounces beef broth [or beef bouillon if you have a brand you like to use]
2 carrots diced
1 cup frozen green peas
1 cup chopped cremini mushrooms
1 tablespoon extra-virgin olive oil
1 1/2 tablespoons all-purpose flour
1 teaspoon chopped fresh thyme, sage, or rosemary [optional]
Salt to taste
Pepper to taste
4 medium potatoes, peeled and chopped into 1-inch chunk
2 tablespoons butter
1/2 cup milk [add more or less as needed]
1 medium or large egg, beaten
1 cup shredded cheddar cheese

Directions
FOR CRUST:
Preheat oven to 375 degrees
Let pie crust thaw, prick lightly with a fork
Bake pie crust for about 15 minutes—just until crust begins brown
Remove from oven and let cool while you complete the mashed potato topping and meat pie filling.

FOR TOPPING:

Boil potatoes until tender. Drain and mash with 2 tablespoons of butter, add milk about ¼ cup at a time and 1 teaspoon of salt. Mix until fluffy. When cooled a little, fold in one beaten egg.

FOR FILLING:

Dice up onions, carrots, and mushrooms. Sauté over medium high heat in EVOO with about a tsp of salt. Add chopped garlic and continue to cook until veggies are 'al dente'—tender but not mushy. Remove the veggie mixture.

Brown hamburger or turkey in the same pot. Add veggie mixture back to pot with 6 ounces of beef broth, fresh herbs if you want to use them, a teaspoon of salt and pepper. Cover pot with a tight-fitting lid and cook over medium heat, stirring occasionally, for about 1o minutes.

Mix 1 ½ tablespoons of all-purpose flour in with the remaining beef broth until all lumps are gone. Raise heat until the meat mixture begins to boil. Slowly add the broth/flour mixture while stirring quickly and continue to stir and boil for about 1 minute. Remove from heat. Fold in the peas.

Spoon the mixture into the cooled pie crust. Pile the mashed potatoes on top of the pie and spread to cover. Sprinkle with shredded cheese.

Bake for about 20 minutes, or until the potatoes brown on top. Let cool for 10 or 15 minutes before serving.

Georgie's Tips

Okay, so, not everyone is going to agree that this recipe ought to be called Shepherd's Pie. If you use beef instead of lamb, this is Cottage Pie to many fans of Shepherd's Pie across the pond. In the U.S., this is a version of what most people grew up calling Shepherd's Pie and many of us have never heard of Cottage Pie. The bottom line—whatever you decide to call it is still just as tasty...the old 'rose by any other name' issue in a meat pie.

The CREAMY MASHED POTATOES recipe featured as a side dish for the Chicken Marsala will work too for the topping. If you have a favorite brand of powdered mashed potatoes, you can use them instead. You'll need to make about 2 0r 3 cups according to directions, depending on how high you want the topping to be. I add the beaten egg because I think it helps the topping bake a little firmer, but you can leave it out if you prefer.

You can skip the crust and use only the filling and topping instead, but I think the crust makes it a real "pie!"

ABOUT THE AUTHOR

Anna Celeste Burke is an award-winning, USA Today bestselling author who enjoys *snooping into life's mysteries with fun, fiction, & food—California style!*

A few words for you from Anna…

Life is an extravaganza! Figuring out how to hang tough and make the most of the wild ride is the challenge. On my way to Oahu, to join the rock musician and high school drop-out I had married in Tijuana, I was nabbed as a runaway. Eventually, the police let me go, but the rock band broke up.

Our next stop: Disney World, where we "worked for the Mouse" as chefs, courtesy of Walt Disney World University Chef's School. More education landed us in academia at The Ohio State University. For decades, I researched, wrote, and taught about many gloriously nerdy topics.

Retired now, I'm still married to the same, sweet guy and live with him near Palm Springs, California. I write the Jessica Huntington Desert Cities Mystery series set here in the Coachella Valley and the Corsario Cove Cozy Mystery Series set in California's Central Coast, The Georgie Shaw Mystery series set in the OC, and coming soon, two new series set in California! Won't you join me? Sign up at: http://desertcitiesmystery.com.

Made in the USA
Columbia, SC
25 May 2021

38446745R00150